THE PENULTIMATE MEN

The Penultimate Men

TALES FROM OUR SAVAGE FUTURE

Nantes
2022

THIS IS A BENT MISSILE BOOK,
PUBLISHED BY PILUM PRESS.

Copyright 2020 by Pilum Press.
Second edition 2022.
All rights reserved.

Cover design and typesetting by Luisa Editorial. Copyediting and proofing by Secret Submersible Services. Vibrancy and bigger forearms by Tarzan and the Riddle of Steel.

ISBN: 978-1-956453-03-4

Spring 2022

FOR RAVEN, WHO FOUGHT THE DARNESS OF
THIS WORLD WITH UNFLAGGING COURAGE AND
RELENTLESS HOPE. AS SHE ISPIRED ALL THOSE
WHO KNEW HER, MAY THIS COLLECTION INSPIRE
YOU, DEAR READER, TO ALWAYS LOOK FOR THE
LIGHT IN EVEN YOUR OWN DARKEST HOURS.

CONTENTS

THE UNIVERSE NEXT DOOR

An introduction

"I can't tell anyone about my story because they'll steal my idea."

Ihave heard the above line a lot over my years of associating with writers, both on-line and in person. These days, being old and cynical and not inclined to waste time in pointless arguments, I just change the subject, thereby frustrating the speaker who was hoping that I would beg her or him for some hints regarding this wonderful million-dollar idea.

If I were in the business of debunking myths, though, I would say something like this: "Nobody is going to steal your idea. Nobody wants to steal your idea because ideas are worthless. Making art isn't about having an idea. Making art is about doing the hard work to turn an idea into something real. The whole concept of a million-dollar idea is pure bullshit. It's a scam dreamed up by movie studio lawyers who do too much coke and need to convince the board of directors that they actually do something to justify their outrageous retainers."

The concept of intellectual property used to be pretty straightforward. If Person A writes a story, or paints a picture, or sings a song, then the creation belongs to Person A. If Person B publishes those particular words or that picture or this recording of that song without paying Person A, Person B is stealing from Person A.

Then lawyers got involved.

Well, it would probably be fairer to say that lawyers' clients got involved. But the upshot is that a straightforward idea ("don't steal other people's work") got turned into a labyrinthine mess where Person C gets to claim that Person A's original creation was somehow based on something that Person C created previously, like Harlan Ellison forcing James Cameron to add a based-on-a-story-by title card at the end of *The Terminator*.

Since it is impossible to prove (or even adequately describe) what goes on in an artist's mind during the act of creation, a cottage industry of claiming intellectual property infringement has grown up. A creative cold war has broken out. Media conglomerates with deep pockets unleash their legal hounds at the first hint that someone else told a story similar to one that they are currently trying to sell to the public. And while there are a lot of reasons why traditionally published genre fiction has become so stale and tired, this fear of mutually-assured legal destruction over "stolen ideas" is certainly a factor.

It didn't used to be this way.

In fact, the whole existence of science fiction as a genre is a direct result of authors stealing each other's ideas. Suppose, for example, that the first person who wrote about a "hyperdrive" as a way of getting around the speed of light limitation—imagine this genius had kept control of the idea and nobody else could use hyperdrive ships in a story for fear of a lawsuit. (I have no clue who this was. Ask Jeffro Johnson.)

Or robots. Or domed cities on the moon. Or human cloning. Suppose that the H. G. Wells estate sued anyone who wrote a story about time travel or invisibility. Or take characters: Robin Hood, the Scarlet Pimpernel, Zorro, The Shadow, and Batman are all essentially the same character. How many hardboiled detective characters are there? How many would there be if Raymond Chandler had sued anyone who based a character on Philip Marlowe? Entire subgenres could have been erased that way. How many Pulp SF stories mentioned Luna City or Marsport or Venusburg? How many pulp heroes carried blasters or vibroblades? And how many fantasy worlds are just Tolkien's Middle Earth with the serial numbers filed off? (If you answered "All of them," you have some reading to do.)

"Ah, but those things are tropes," you say. "Conventions of the genre."

Yes, they are. That's what tropes are—ideas that got stolen in the days before stealing ideas was a thing. Why do zombies eat living human brains? Because Dan O'Bannon had been struggling with managing chronic pain while he was making a movie and happened to learn from his doctor that the chemicals that mask pain are produced in the brain. He reasoned that the living dead are in constant pain from their decaying bodies, and the only way to stop it was to ingest endorphins from the living. Watch the director's commentary on *Return of the Living Dead*—he explains it. This great idea has passed into the zombie mythology as a trope. But it came from one particular filmmaker who put it into one particular film.

While most good ideas that we know as tropes aren't so easily identified; they all came from someplace. Somebody thought of them first. And gave them away. During the first three-quarters or so of the twentieth century—the time during which science fiction and fantasy (and horror and crime fiction and all of the sub-types and hybrids) were becoming real literature in terms of sales (if not in terms of academic respectability) everybody understood that it was the work that mattered, not the idea.

Authors read each other's stories and built on them. Every new story spawned a dozen new ones as authors thought "Well, that was interesting, but what if you took that idea and went that way instead?" It wasn't called stealing in those days. It was called inspiration. Sometimes an homage or a pastiche, if you want to get continental about it. It was how the business worked, and it's how we went from *The First Men In The Moon* to *First Lensman* in barely a generation.

The cyberpunk movement of the 1980s briefly recaptured that kind of cooperative worldbuilding, with writers like Bruce Sterling and Walter Jon Williams and William Gibson hammering out an imaginary future together. But consider—we are now living in the time that the original cyberpunk stories were set in, and we're still writing stories set in the mythical 2020 imagined by the writers of 1980. The present has actually outstripped science fiction in terms of modernity.

That's intolerable.

And that's the best science fiction has to offer. The genre has become overrun with various flavors of retrofuturism: steampunk, dieselpunk, atomic age science fiction, space operas settings that Flash Gordon would recognize. We've gotten to the point where the only way forward is to go back. Not just to the style and spirit of the pulps, but the sense of community, of shared exploration into the unknown. And for that, in today's litigious society, we need shared worlds, what Rawle Nyanzi calls "open-source intellectual properties". We need authors who are willing to give active consent to sharing their ideas. What was once taken for granted needs to be stated explicitly.

It's not that difficult. I've done it myself, with the *Eldritch Earth* setting. And while that project didn't exactly set the world on fire, I think it was a qualified success, with a half dozen or so authors all building on the basic concept (which, to be honest, I stole myself from H. P. Lovecraft and Edgar Rice Burroughs.)

And here we have it again. A setting that was originally a game (one that I played in myself, to give full disclosure). While the world comes straight out of the 1970s, you can feel a certain synergy in the stories, a growing together, a willingness to share. The stories that follow are not set in exactly the same world, not in the sense that the *Thieves' World* and *Wild Cards* collections had a strict continuity. Instead, they can be seen as variations on a theme, or impressionistic paintings of the same subject. The individual authors expanded on the original setting, added their own flourishes, and created something new. Jon Mollison's superhero-like mutant warriors in "Wind On the Water" are a different breed than the strange unfortunate creatures in Neal Durando's "Root Hog or Die". Sky Hernstrom brings his own characters Mortu and Kyrus, into the shared universe. Or possibly Hernstrom brings the shared setting into Mortu and Kyrus's world. There's an innate flexibility to this kind of collection, a kind of Rube Goldberg, kitchen sink aesthetic where incongruity is a feature, not a bug.

It's the famous "what if" thought experiment that characterizes the best and most original science fiction. What if you add humanoid badgers and mutant superpowers to a naval battle? What if demon hunters drove a classic muscle car? How would a coming-of-age vision quest work in a radioactive wasteland? If a two-headed pig could talk, what would it say?

Try it and find out.

Or to quote e e cummings, "listen: there's a hell of a good universe next door; let's go."

—Misha Burnett, 15 November 2019

FIRE AND FOLLY

Jon Mollison

Spearshaker, cross-legged in his furs, rested motionless save for his alert and watchful eyes. He scanned the rim of the amphitheater and found no sign of eavesdroppers. A spark of hope flared in his heart that they might complete the evening's business uninterrupted.

Across the fire sat Ox, nearly largest and cleverest of the boys, and certainly the most respected by the boys and men alike. The largest boy, seated to Ox's right, was far from the cleverest. What Big Belly lacked in cunning and patience he tried to make up for in strength and ferocity. He generally succeeded too, but as this group of boys grew and learned the ways of the city dwellers, Big Belly's authority over the rest waned even as Ox's waxed. Frustrated, but understanding the ways of their people, Big Belly grudgingly gave way to Ox over the years. Tonight he went so far as to arrive early to secure the best seat around the fire for Ox. This was an impressive sacrifice that allayed Spearshaker's concerns over the boy's future. Should he survive the journey ahead, Big Belly's strength and loyalty would prove a valuable asset.

Once every year, on a cool autumn night, the world shrank to a bright warm fire surrounded by a small circle of faces, all smooth and fresh save for that of the Spearshaker. All on the cusp of adulthood. Around and above the circle the bones of the old world rose, a lattice of thick metal beams, reached up hundreds of feet into the night sky.

The fire burned at the bottom of a hollow sunk a full story beneath the surrounding land. The stones that once filled the lattice had been plundered over the centuries to build tidy houses that now clustered around and within the bones of other, smaller, steel skeletons. Tiers of stone had been carefully placed around the perimeter of the basement to create a small amphitheater large enough to seat the entire community, though in recent decades latecomers were forced to clamber up into the lower reaches of the steel frame for a view of the proceedings.

Tonight, the people of Gateway huddled in their warm, tidy homes. Were it not for the men on the city walls who scanned the horizon for trouble, these twenty boys and one tired old man would have been alone. The boys sat breathless with anticipation of their impending adventure. The old man, weary with the knowledge that tonight would be the last day he would see them all numbered among the living, sat and watched their innocent excitement. Like boys had done from time immemorial they jostled and shoved and taunted each other in shows of quiet challenge and braggadocio.

He knew not all would return.

Spearshaker took in other faces in the ring. The cruel, mocking eyes of Howler. The warm and reassuring earnestness of Heartstrong as he whispered encouragement to his best friend, the soft and skittish Jumper. All reminded Spearshaker of others who had come before, of boys present on previous nights, and he reminded himself not to invest too much in any of them. His soul bore more scars than his aging body, and he tried in vain to steel it against further hurt. Preparing them for the coming trials was difficult enough as it was—keeping these boys at arm's length was his armor against the pain of loss sure to come. In all his years of preparing the boys of the city for the ordeal, he had yet to experience a year where all returned to the city alive. Every year piled fresh burdens upon his already heavy load of sorrow.

He paused to meet the direct gaze of Stillwater, the best woodsman in the group, whose spirit had rankled from a young age at the indignity of being confined within the city walls. Here was the one boy present that Spearshaker knew would return to his city of birth, beneath the bones of the old world. The boy had taken to fieldcraft and hunting like a fish to water. So much so that he often spent his nights ghosting through the ruins outside the wall, curious about the extensive rubble that lay beneath the blanket of countless years of nature's green onslaught. The harrowing journey would be as difficult for Stillwater as for the rest, but alone among the group did Spearshaker find eyes that understood what was to come. His eyes, too old to be set into a face so young, carried an appreciation of the night's import and also, somehow, a touch of sympathy for Spearshaker.

The old man snorted in amused surprise. He had suffered this night every year for two decades. In all those years he had never experienced such understanding and empathy from a boy. Boys were too full of youth and boasts and questions to spare a thought for the haggard man seated before the fire. At the sound of his snort, the boys hushed their conversations and turned his way.

Spearshaker cleared this throat and spared a glance to the boy seated directly to his left. Seated on the smallest and least comfortable rock, farthest from the fire, the smallest of them idly drew in the dirt with a long stick. Foxtrot bore the brunt of years of teasing from the others with quiet dignity. Unlike few others around the fire, he responded to the practical jokes and testing shoves with a friendly acceptance that had won him quiet supporters, even as it ensured his place at the bottom of their hierarchy. Unlike Howler's whining protests and accusations of the unfairness of his frequent losses, Foxtrot always picked himself up and retreated into himself or, as he preferred, his father's books. This one, Spearshaker thought, reminded him all too much of himself at that age.

He shook himself as a dog rids himself of water after a swim. With a grunt, he settled himself back upon the smooth earth-covered floor before the fire.

"Tomorrow you leave Gateway as boys," Spearshaker intoned. "You will return to us as men." He paused and met each of their eyes in turn. "Or your bones will join with the millions scattered about the countryside."

The boys responded to the challenge as fit their nature, by puffing up their chests, or blinking away fears, or staring into the fire. "The moon has already set," Spearshaker continued. "Without its light to guide your way, your journey will be more difficult. You must choose to travel blind by night or face the dangers of the day. The animals and the savages who prowl the wilderness that separates our fair city from the cities of other civilized men know the seasons. They will be alert to your passage. Travel fast by day, or crawl by night, this first decision is yours and yours alone. I am not here to teach you how to survive the dangers of the wilds. You have spent your youth learning how to recognize and avoid them. I am here to tell you about the dangers of the old world," he glanced up at the spider-web of steel rising overhead. "And something of how it fell. That we might not repeat the mistakes of our forefathers.

"You have waited long enough. But before you hear the sad tale of how the men who built these came to ruin," he gestured up and around him, raising both hands and eyes to encompass the rust-colored steel frame. He allowed them a moment to reflect on the heights those men of old had reached before dropping his hands and returning them to the present. "You deserve to learn of your fate. In consultation with your fathers, and with the Council, and with all of the men of the city, I have selected a destination for each of you."

The night grew silent but for the crackle of the fire and, far off, the chorus of wolves in the night. The boys leaned in, staring intently at Spearshaker, and hung on his every word. Behind each rested a pile of supplies, a water skin, a pack of food and small tools, a blanket, and blades and bows to guard them. A second pack contained trade goods, small luxuries they would present to their hosts in far off cities should they survive the long and arduous trek.

In the coming weeks, boys from surrounding cities would arrive in Gateway to present gifts of their own. The boys around the fire had seen the strangers arrive in years past and watched them leave, each with one of the city girls on his arm. Now it was their turn to strike out, prove their mettle, and if they could survive the dangers and convince their hosts of their worth, return with a woman of their own.

A few, Stillwater and Foxtrot among them, understood the purpose of the harrowing journey. Heartstrong, the son of a shepherd and familiar with the rudiments of animal husbandry, likely grasped the concept better than the others. The rest? Spearshaker could see the lustful gleam in their eyes as they anticipated finally slaking that particular thirst openly, rather than through stolen moments with the village girls. Already they were looking past the dangers to come, a dangerous thing on the eve of their journey.

Spearshaker flung a handful of black dust into the fire. Brilliant sparks flared bright white and shot into the sky, startling them all.

"Listen!" Spearshaker shouted, capturing their full attention. "Your whole lives have been spent safe within the confines of Gateway—even outside of the wall; you have been protected by the bravery and strength of the men of your tribe. Tomorrow you travel alone. Should you stumble and fall, there will be no help for you no matter how loud you cry out. Tomorrow, for the first time in your lives, it will be you against the world. Do not take this journey lightly. Even one small mistake can prove your last. Imagine if that mistake occurs when your new brides are with you! Eh? What then? What will become of her? Of the city that needs your strength?" He looked at Ox and Big Belly. "Your cunning?" He looked at Stillwater and Foxtrot. "Your knowledge?" He looked at Heartstrong. "Your children?" He looked at them all. "It is not just trinkets you carry with you. You carry the future of Gateway on your backs. Do not forget. You are men of the city—not savages like the country dwellers. Be swift. Be brave. And return to us as men."

The boys rocked back under the intensity of his voice, even the most cocksure of them cowed by his outburst. Spearshaker sighed and settled back onto his backside. With a jerk of his chin he started with Ox, "North to The City of Winds." Then Big Belly, "East to Crossroads." Strongheart, "West to Fountains". Jumper started when he announced, "South to the City on the Bluffs." Before Strongheart could interrupt, he continued, "Yes, you may travel via the Wide River, but you may not take one of the city's rafts. You must construct your own outside the city walls."

With the wave of his hand, Spearshaker indicated other boys and named smaller settlements in every direction. Foxtrot he directed to journey toward the City of Music, and for the first time offered more than just a place name. "You are to remain there for two years, learn what you can from them, and return with as much knowledge of their ways as you can. Your pack is heavier than most, laden with books," at the boy's sudden smile he held up one hand. "Books you have already read, mind you, containing much of our knowledge of animal husbandry. Leave them and return with a head full of their wisdom, and a woman to share your burden." The young man settled back but could not wipe the smile from his face. To be allowed to remain in a foreign city for as long as a year was a mark of honor and showed that the Council held high hopes for him to bring the light of new music to their city. Little did he suspect that he was contributing to a larger project designed to unravel the mystery of the common ancestry of all of the cities. The knowledge he carried would help shrink the cultural gap that had grown between Music City and Gateway. With enough Foxtrots thrown at the issue, one day the men of the cities might even be able to rebuild the legendary empire that once stretched from sea to shining sea, as one fragment of song passed down through the generations put it.

Finally, Spearshaker turned to the last of the boys. Stillwater.

Around them, the first rush of whispered conversations grew silent again. Momentarily forgetting themselves in the excitement of learning their destination, the boys had begun the congratulations and teasing early. Only after several long moments in which Spearshaker could not bring himself to speak did they realize that Foxtrot's destination was not the most striking.

One by one, they nudged each other and jerked their heads toward Stillwater, who sat placidly watching Spearshaker's long face. When the circle grew quiet again, he finally announced, "The Apple."

A silent wave of shock spread around the circle. With quiet amazement, the boys looked about to reassure themselves that they had heard right. Stillwater merely closed his eyes.

The destination—a massive, ghost-haunted ruin—lay across the Wide River, across the plains and over mountains, beyond wide swamps and even unto the uttermost east where skeletal towers huddled together on a long island the legends held to be the source of the calamity that saw the fall of the old world. No boy had ever been sent to a destination so far away. Even Ox, the biggest and bravest of them, was merely sent to the big lake in the north—a dangerous journey and one few begrudged him, but nothing like the Apple. It would take months to journey there and return, and all during the long, bleak winter months. Stillwater could not even seek shelter in the numerous cities along the way. He would have to skirt Arch City, Iron City, Liberty, and countless smaller cities in between. It was a nearly impossible task, and every boy around the warm fire half-suspected it to be a death sentence for some terrible crime Stillwater must have committed in secret.

A long, slow sigh was the only sign he gave that he understood. Then he opened his eyes and nodded.

"Your pack contains messages from the far western cities. Historical information we have copied into our library and which must be added to the records kept in the cloistered abbeys of The Apple. Eventually, these texts will filter out through the rest of civilization, and so help us rebuild what we have lost. Your journey will speed mankind along the path of reconstruction. The Council knows you face a heavy risk, and they would not laden you with it if they even suspected you might bend under its weight. Unlike the rest, you will earn your manhood upon reaching The Apple, and you will return to us free to choose your own path. As a man."

Every soul in Gateway knew Stillwater yearned to wander the world. As a boy, he had always sought to learn what was over the next hill, but there was no next hill capable of satisfying his curiosity once and for all. By offering the boy manhood on arrival at The Apple, the tribe was offering him the freedom to leave Gateway and take his valuable hunting and tracking skills with him. While savages roamed freely outside of the city, it was the rare civilized man indeed who courted that hazard willingly.

And yet, men like that did exist. A few wanderers bounced from city to city, sharing news and trinkets and stories and songs as they wished. Such men were hardened and given a place of honor at the fire in any city. Romantic heroes, and few in number, they were the stuff of legends. With a few years seasoning, Spearshaker mused, Stillwater would fit right in.

"Remember who you are," Spearshaker told the circle of glowing faces. "You are descendants of the men who built these cities. Unlike the savages outside the walls, you have not turned your back on God or wisdom or your fellow man. Remember your lessons, and the virtues we have tried to instill in you. Be brave and prudent, do not lose hope, and you will survive. Some of you have already laid the foundation stones for your homes, a good sign of your faith in better days to come. When you are cold and alone and surrounded by barbarians, think of the warm home to come, filled with strong children and a loyal wife. Think of your friends," he waved to the boys seated around the fire, "who await your return, and with whom you will grow old and ugly and cranky and hairy," he scratched his long beard, eliciting laughs, "and with whom you will help mankind reclaim his birthright. These thoughts will strengthen your resolve and remind you that you are never truly alone. You are always accompanied by the hopes and dreams of your friends and indeed those of every citizen of Gateway. Think on this." Spearshaker sat back in silence and allowed the long minutes of quiet to slowly give way to the boy's restlessness. Their voices gradually rose as they first whispered boasts of how soon they would return to Gateway and speculated on the curves and demeanor of the brides they would bring with them. He allowed them a few moments of anticipation before grudgingly drawing their attention away from the future and back to the present, to steer their thoughts even farther back into the mist-shrouded days of the past. Softly, he reminded them of the second purpose of his fireside sermon. "Before you leave, on this journey that could well be your last, you deserve to learn the closely guarded secret of mankind's downfall."

Once more the boys fell silent. Instead of the anticipated long-winded lecture, Spearshaker asked them a question.

"How many of you sit here around the fire?"

"Nineteen," came the immediate soft reply from the small boy on his left. Foxtrot's eyes never left the dwindling flames of the fire, yet he answered before many of the boys even understood that the nature of the fireside circle had changed.

"And how many girls of your age live among us?"

"Twenty-two," Foxtrot answered.

"Nearly the same number," Spearshaker observed.

"Almost," Strongheart picked up the thread. "We would be twenty-one here tonight, but Yellowtop died beneath the hooves of old Crankeye's bull three summers back."

Not to be outdone, Ox interrupted, "And not two moons ago Beavertooth died defending his household when those nomads snuck over the wall and slit his father's throat."

A low growl echoed around the fire. The boys well remembered that terrible night—the fear and confusion and flames, the shouts of alarm and wail of women's voices. Most of the naked barbarians had been hunted down and slaughtered like the animals they were. Beavertooth's decision to sound the alarm had cost him his life. It also saved his mother and two sisters. Not for the first time, the boys had learned of the savagery and cunning of the men who roamed the wilds outside the city walls. And not for the first time, they were reminded of the price and reward of sacrifice for the city. They each had a family of their own, and each hoped to show as much courage as Beavertooth had on his last night alive.

"Before them," Foxtrot softly added, "Mossrock drowned in the river and Cloudy dashed his brains out when he fell out of a high tree."

Even as the boy's thoughts turned toward memories of their fallen friends, Spearshaker reminded them of others. "How many died of the Red Pocks before you were old enough to remember them? And the Barking Cough? Fen would be here too, but for the disease that left him crippled."

Impatient, Big Belly prodded the old man, "The world is a dangerous place. We get it."

"The year of your birth the city saw fifty-three other babies take their first breath, twenty-nine of them boys. Tonight, just nineteen remain, and by the next full moon that number will be further diminished. Of the

twenty six girls born, all but four have survived—twenty-two now sleep soundly in their
beds."

Spearshaker intended to allow the boys
a moment to consider this vital point, but a
shrill laugh called out from above. The clatter
of loose stones echoed about the small amphitheater, and the boys turned to look over
Spearshaker's shoulder where two shadows
emerged from the night.

Spearshaker's shoulders sagged, and he
pinched the bridge of his nose. He had hoped
tonight would pass without this added misery.

"Nineteen," the forward figure snapped, acid
in her voice. The firelight brought her face into
focus as she descended the steps of the amphitheater, eliciting a groan from the boys.

Hickory. Headstrong and feisty, the girl had
earned her childname thanks to a relentless-
ly bitter temperament. A strong-jawed tomboy
not entirely unpleasing to the eye, the boys
around the fire had long since tired of her
acrimonious carriage and incessant demands
to join in their leisure time exploration of the
hills and woods near the city walls. For her, everything was a contest. She ruined the thrill of
practice runs of their coming journey, in which
they experimented and failed and learned in
safety and mutual support, by turning them
into games of one-upmanship. She constantly
goaded them into taking stupid risks. Worst
of all were her constant efforts to challenge
them, to prove that she was one of them and

capable of following their every step, despite her obvious physical and temperamental shortcomings.

Still young, and wholly without the benefit of wisdom, the boys had struggled to cope with her demand that she be counted as one of them, which was made worse by her frequent retreats into the protected status of all the women of Gateway. Even Ox, who wore the mantle of leadership as comfortably as his own skin, often found himself confounded at her games. He could not simply bludgeon her into submission the way he had Big Belly and Howler and even several boys a year or two his senior.

Worst of all was the way she played them, one off the other, constantly offering promises of hidden affections or threatening to spread rumors about them amongst the rest of the girls. Even the knowledge that they were destined to find wives among the surrounding cities was no defense against her games. The girl vexed them in every way they could imagine and a few they couldn't. Most of the boys considered the notion of leaving Hickory and her games well behind them to be one small benefit of their coming dangerous journey into the wilds.

At Hickory's side, a half-step behind her, walked the wide-hipped but plain-faced Yoe. A quiet and lonely girl, she had fallen into Hickory's wake in a vain effort to find the kind of camaraderie that came naturally to other girls. Disinclined to the frivolous pastimes the men of the city worked so hard to provide, the girl had kept to herself until pulled into Hickory's orbit. Unlike the slender girl at her side, whose thrust back shoulders and high chin conveyed a sense of belligerent determination, Yoe walked with shoulders sagged and peered out at the world from behind straight-cut bangs that half-hid her darting eyes.

Upon reaching the bottom of the amphitheater steps, Hickory chuckled. She waved dismissively at the horizon around them and sneered, "Nineteen silly little girls lay waiting in those cities. And for what? For one of you boys to waltz in through their gates and carry them off to his own city forever?" She spat on the ground. Instead of shoving her way into the circle, she began to pace around the boys, forcing them to crane their necks to follow her progress or ignore her altogether. With her entrance, the mood of the boys had shifted. No longer jocular and full of excitement, the boys turned sullen.

"You don't belong here," Ox rumbled.

"We're preparing for our passage," Big Belly added.

"You think you are the only ones who want out of this prison?" Hickory sneered at the boys as she stalked around them. "You think us too frail and weak? We're each stronger than him." The last word dripped with contempt as she pointed an accusatory finger at Foxtrot.

The boy stiffened at the insult, but his eyes

never left the fire.

"We are clever and stealthy enough to slip out of our homes," the girl continued. "We have listened to your little ceremony from the beginning, and none of you even suspected we were there." At this, all of the boys shifted uncomfortably. "With vigilance so lax, none of you will last until the end of the week, and you all know I'm better with a bow than Howler."

"The ones you can pull, anyway," Howler retorted. The sly reference to the smaller bow that was all her arms and shoulders could draw brought her up short even as the chuckle from the boys broke some of the tension generated by her appearance. Once she had been as strong as any of them, but as puberty raced through their numbers like a plague, she found herself quickly left behind by all but the smallest of the boys. She had never forgiven either them or the world for the unfairness of it all. And now she meant to repay the boys for nature's cruelties by ruining the last night of their childhood.

Before the laughter could die down, and before Hickory could issue a hot reply, Spearshaker held up one hand. He pointed to the lowest tier of the stone seats around them and ordered the girls to sit. "If you want to prove yourself, then I will assign you a destination— wait." The last word he barked as an order that brooked no objection. The boys had all inhaled to voice their opposition to this breach of custom.

"We were discussing the fall of the old

world," Spearshaker cut them off. "We will finish that discussion, and then if the girls still want to prove their manhood," he waited a beat for the boys to laugh and the girls to fume, "then by their appearance here they accept the risks and dangers. So be it. We were discussing the fall of the old world."

Out of the corner of his eye, he watched the two girls wrap their cloaks around their shoulders. The cold stone of the amphitheater was too far from the fire to receive much warmth, but they counted their continued presence as a sign of victory. They could stay, in their minds, each just one of the guys.

"More boys were born in your year," Spearshaker resumed his lesson, "as in every year. But fewer boys survived to this day. Why?"

"We take more risks," Ox supplied.

"And why is that?"

From the stone bench, Hickory sulked, "Because you won't let girls do it."

Instead of correcting her, Spearshaker nodded his shaggy head. "It is not encouraged, which often seems like disallowing. Set that aside—why do the men of the cities push boys to take risks when they do not push girls in the same way? Why do we send our boys out into the wilds and not our girls?"

Big Belly slapped his stomach and then his arms. "Because we are stronger."

"Not all of you," Hickory sneered.

Foxtrot's mouth twisted, but he said nothing.

"In part," Spearshaker agreed. "But there is

more to it. Consider what the men of the city bring to our community and compare that to what the women bring."

"A warm dinner?"

Spearshaker did not see who suggested that but laughed in spite of himself. "Let's try this from another angle. What do women provide for the city that men cannot?"

"Children," Stillwater spoke up for the first time.

Foxtrot saw the deeper answer. "Our future. If every boy here dies this night, the women of our year can still bring forth the children. If every woman of our year dies…"

"Our city dies," Spearshaker concluded.

Heads nodded in the firelight. The boys had seen the same math play out in the herds of cattle and sheep that grazed in the ruin-spotted meadows around the city. The animals were culled when young, and so long as a few males survived to the winter, the next spring would see a wealth of new livestock enter the fields. They had never heard the same math applied to humans before but instantly understood the significance.

"So boys don't matter," Howler said with an accusing tone to his voice. "We save the women because they are more important. That's why we have to risk our lives to journey to other cities? Because our deaths are no big loss?"

Spearshaker held his tongue as Ox shook his head and answered the question for him. "It is not about importance. Each is important in his or her own way. It is about proving your worth to the city. The women have worth insofar as they bear and raise the young children—even those without children of their own help provide care, do they not? Just as every man provides what he can. Even Fen, whose twisted legs prevent him from leaving the city—he will never take a wife, and will never stand watch on the wall, but his years of copying the old texts onto fresh paper prove his worth. Does anyone here doubt that?"

The boys collectively murmured agreement with the sentiment, but Hickory could not hold her tongue. "So that's it then? Women are to be brood mares and nothing more?" She barked another snide laugh. "I've got better things to do with my time."

"If you think ensuring the survival of our people is not worth your time," Spearshaker sighed, "then go with the Council's blessing. You won't be missed." After a beat, he said, "Railsplitterhome."

In the faint light, Spearshaker saw Hickory's perpetual scowl tighten. Reaching the small settlement of Railsplitterhome, the home of a great and powerful old world king, was half the distance any of the boys had been assigned. The relatively safe journey represented an intentional slight, but a journey she dared not refuse as it also represented an acquiescence to her demand.

Hickory shot to her feet and snapped, "Fine!" With a whirl, she flounced up the steps of the amphitheater and called out, "Come on, Yoe. We'll be back before any of you even reach your cities."

Yoe sat for a moment. She slowly stood and made her way up the stairs of the theater. After only a few steps, she paused and turned. She peeked out from beneath her long bangs and hesitated. Her voice trembled as she asked, "Do I… Is it…?"

Spearshaker offered a warm and understanding smile. "If you can sneak back into your bed without waking your family…" He shot a look of warning around the fire, "It will be as though you were never here tonight." Taking their cue, the boys nodded their agreement.

Yoe sighed with relief even as Hickory, waiting at the top of the steps, cried out to her. "I hope the man who comes for you is hideous," she cursed her betrayer. "Maybe I'll reach Railsplitterhome and just keep on walking." She grabbed her cloak and pulled it close as she stormed off into the cold autumn night.

"Do you think she will return to us?" Strongheart asked. Spearshaker shrugged and sighed. "If you see her along the way…"

"Don't worry," the boy interrupted. "She wants to prove herself; I won't get in her way. Are we nearly done? I'm eager to get started."

"Yes," Foxtrot agreed. "You meant to tell us what happened to the old world. Something about the ratio of boys and girls?"

The boy was sharp, Spearshaker thought.

He might not be the swiftest or the strongest, but he was sharp enough. Spearshaker had once followed Foxtrot into the wilds and watched as the boy cached extra supplies for tonight's trip. Unlike the rest of them, he had begun his preparations months ago. Smart. He would be fine, Spearshaker decided.

"We inherited a dangerous world," Spearshaker finally answered. "Our forefathers did not. Their technology enabled them to create a world where the only danger men faced came from other men. As a result of their wealth and safety, they found themselves with a surfeit of women, women who failed to understand that the world around them did not stop being hostile when the men around them conquered both nature and the surrounding tribes."

The following silence was broken by Foxtrot, who helped the boys understand by musing, "Cities full of Hickories."

They shuddered at the thought.

Spearshaker nodded. "She would have raised fine children, strong-willed like her, but despite her claims, she is not one of you. She does not think like you. She thinks with this," he placed a hand over his heart. "Instead of this," he moved his hand to place one finger on his forehead. "Some of you were like that once." He looked Big Belly in the eyes. "But over time you learned that this," his hand fell back to his heart, "tells you only about yourself. The wolf and the nomad do not care what this contains. To escape their jaws, you must learn to use this," his hand went back to his head. "Your head must control your emotions. You learned this at play while wrestling in the dirt and while exploring the world outside our walls.

"This Beavertooth understood before he died, and so he died not as a boy, but as a man. The night of his death, his heart was no doubt filled with fear and told him to feign sleep, but he did not listen to those doubts. He gave up his own life to save those of his mother and sisters, and at that moment, he became a man. He lived as a boy, but he died as a man. Just as any of you who die along the path to your destination will die as a man.

"Nature does not care if you feel ready." He packed as much contempt into that word as he could. "If you are ready, you will survive. If you are not, you won't. As men, you must accept the world for what it is, and not what you feel it should be. All the pleading and emoting in the world won't save you from the jaws of the wildcat.

"A hard lesson and one Hickory will learn too late, just as the men of the old world learned too late to prevent their downfall."

"So that's it, then?" Big Belly scratched his round stomach, a nervous tic that betrayed his confusion. "Women did this to us?"

"No!" For the first time, Spearshaker's voice rose in anger. "If a child begs for a toy you know he will break, and you give it to him, is it the child's fault the toy was broken?"

No answer interrupted the crackle of the slowly dying flames. None was necessary, as every boy understood where the real fault lay and steeled himself not to repeat the mistakes of the men of the old world. Until a small voice from his left spoke up. "Hickory will die out there in the wilds, Spearshaker." Foxtrot turned his head to face the old man. "Is her death your fault?"

A look of sorrow descended upon Spearshaker's bearded face.

"Yes."

WIND ON THE WATER

Jon Mollison

"Come back to me," she said. Wind stood at the door of their small cabin, dressed in his furs and leathers, sword belt on and bow in hand. His scramble to dress and arm himself had awakened his wife. She sat up in bed, wool blanket clutched in two fists held to her chin. Her eyes shone in the crimson glow of the last few dying coals.

He looked to the wide bed on the opposite side of the cozy one room cabin, the widest bed in the village, and the six children tangled within its blankets. So innocent and fragile.

Of the eight in his family, only he had felt the silent press of Empath's sending: Attack!

He nodded. "I'll try. Pray for me."

He left the warmth of home and slipped

out into the frigid outdoor air. Standing on the small covered porch of his quiet little home, he felt his wife's fear echo in his heart.

During the night, an early spring had succumbed to one last tantrum from Father Winter. A thin blanket of snow covered the ground, the trees, and the village buildings. Only the gray waters of the vast lake lay unchanged by the snowfall.

In the thin light of an overcast dawn, he raced down the lane among the village buildings, low rings of stone capped by high cones of thatch. The normally muddy lane shone white with snow in the early morning starlight, marred only by several lines of black boot prints, all headed for the stone church at the end of the lane.

So many tracks. At least one set from each house, with two or more departing from homes with sons old enough to stand and fight.

She hated these moments, when danger appeared on the horizon and duty ripped him from her side. Every time he answered that call, she called him back. And every time she did so, thoughts of his warm bed and the quiet sighs of his children and a few private moments in his wife's warm embrace before the little ones woke tempted him to turn back.

He followed in the dark prints pressed into the snow. All of them pointed toward whatever danger threatened the village. None of them pointed back toward the comfort of hearth and home.

His breath steaming as he hurried down the lane, he realized the tracks did not depart from every home after all. Mostly from the homes of men who worked the boats, with only a few exceptions. That meant a waterborne attack. An attack this early in the spring? The swamp rats didn't usually send their ironclad out on the lake until the risk of winter storms had faded.

Strange days.

Around the corner, a crowd waited at the base of the church steps. All sailors and fighters, but he also saw Claws, Doubletime, and Threesixty. Odd. Though craftsmen, they were three of the best warriors in the village, and each fought well on the slippery decks of the boats.

Held in reserve, perhaps? If the boats couldn't drive off the attackers, somebody would have to delay them on the beaches long enough to allow the women and children to dash for the safety of Eau Claire. Empath allowed most of the landlubbers rest until the boats were in the water. Smart. It would let the ships set sail without the confusion of tearful wives and rowdy children underfoot.

"Now we know why they call you Wind and not Speed, eh?" Handy clapped his upper right hand on Wind's shoulder as he joined the crowd. The two friends shared a grim smile, then joined the crowd in craning their necks up toward the church cupola. Beyond the church, they had a clear view of the lake, which lay at the bottom of a short bluff and across a hundred or so yards of beach and white plains. The broken breakwater that guided a broad and lazy river out into the lake was coated with white snow. A faint westerly breeze pushed gentle waves up the breakwater, but not enough to disturb the blanket of white.

TWELVE SQUARE. BLUE AND WHITE. HEADED OUR WAY.

Empath rarely sent more than a single word. And never to so many men gathered at the foot of the stone church. He had to be exhausted up in that cold and exposed belfry.

A few men, farmers whose homes lay inland from the village, but who possessed some experience on the water, puffed up to join the crowd, and just missed Empath's long message.

The crowd jostled as they rushed in a mob down the stone steps that carried them from the bluff to the river, where their lake boats lay tied up along the ancient steel bulwark that held back the river on this side. The steel pilings on the opposite bank had fallen years ago, prey to the trees that rushed in to take advantage of the abandoned settlement. Only silent trees and dark shadows faced the boats from that direction. Downriver, civilization slumbered, but here and now, war had come.

Wind allowed the fighting men to go down first, and stood at the top of the steps, explaining to the last few arrivals, "Racine, from the sounds of things. Twelve ships, headed straight for us."

A passing farmer, gnarled with the passage of years, blinked two pair of eyes in confusion. He muttered, "Their king should know better. We taught his dad to steer clear of our waters when I was a boy."

"Strange days," Wind answered.

Another farmer's lower mouth chuckled ruefully, steam blowing in the cold air as his upper mouth said, "Is there any other kind?"

Wind waited for the last of them to pass before following the crowd down the stone stairs, now slick with mashed and melted snow. He could wait. His role was far from the front line. His little outrigger with its simple triangular sail was built for speed and endurance, so his task was to observe from afar and scurry away north to notify the Havenites and the Dutchmen in the event they too needed to put ships on the water.

When at last Wind arrived at the line of boats moored along the quay, men still scrambled about to prepare the fishing vessels for a fight. They piled nets along the gunwales in thick bundles to guard against arrows. Some sharpened blades. In the ropes above, still others doubled up the rigging. To his surprise, his *Little Abundance* bobbed in the water, ready and waiting for him. He had left it buttoned up tight the previous day. Now the tarp that protected it from the snow had been removed and stowed. The sail loosed. And in the bow of the ship stood Handy.

"Twomind kicked me off his ship for this one," Handy grinned and offered up an oar.

"Said he wants us to meet them first, see if they will parley. He gave me the signal flags while you were shilly-shallying down the hill."

"Couldn't ask for a better partner," Wind said. He smiled back and hopped aboard. In moments, they had loosed the line, shoved away from the steel pilings, and rowed out into the current of the sluggish river. With Handy's four arms and strong back, they were first to leave the river mouth. Into the open water, they paused to drop sail, then lent their efforts to that of the breeze.

A breath of relief escaped from Wind the moment he saw the blue and white square-cut sails with his own eyes. An invasion of the men from the western shores was unexpected, but it was a fight far preferable to facing the black ship from the south.

They made easy time, one stroke from Wind for every two from Handy. Although smaller than the ships they had left behind, the *Little Abundance* was swift, and with three oars in the water lending aid to the wind, they could be assured of reaching the invading fleet first.

Away to the north, they spotted red triangular sails of the South Haven fleet. They headed toward the invaders at an oblique angle. Their approach meant that the Havenites had seen the approaching Racine fleet, and at a greater distance than Empath had. If they were here already, they must have been in their boats before Wind had said goodbye to Abundance. Probably that fellow they had with the bulging eyes. Rumor had it he could see over the horizon with his insect-like orbs. Whatever the reason, their approach heralded an easier fight.

Like the ships of the village, the Havenites sailed in wide-bellied single-masted ships. At this distance, their lateen-rigged mainsails and forward-pointed jib sails looked like flying wedges cutting the horizon. The Havenites carved their bowsprits like spirals, an odd look to Wind's eye. His village preferred their ships to lead with forward jutting, square-cut wood only carved at the tip into the shape of an open hand, palm down in a gesture designed to placate the unpredictable waves of the wide freshwater lake. The westerly breeze that forced the *Little Abundance* to tack back and forth to make headway troubled the Havenites little as they raced to aid to their brothers in the Concord.

Wind turned his attention back to the approaching blue and white sails. "Something odd here," Wind mused. "Why would one of the cities of the Kingdom attack the Concord? And with their entire fleet? I told you the fading of the jewels in the moon was an ill omen?"

Handy gasped and ignored the question. His attention stayed focused on driving the small ship through the still, dark waters of the lake toward a horizon on which sat twelve square sails of blue and white vertical stripes.

"We outnumber them two to one," Wind boasted. "If Bridgman's ships arrive in time, the odds will be even better. What are they thinking?"

Handy shrugged, too exhausted to speak. Once Wind judged that the approaching sails had grown large enough—he could make out prows of each ship and even the rearing dragons painted upon them—he ordered Handy, who sat before him in the small outrigger canoe, "Oars up." Two strokes later, he slapped his oar down and sent a small spritz of icy water onto his friend's right arms.

"My ship, I'm the captain. Oars up, sailor." That did the trick. Handy slumped in his seat. The sprint had taken a lot out of him, but it had also warmed them both up.

Wind kept driving his own oar into the water as he explained. "We have a good enough head start on the other boats, and I want you fresh in case we need to run."

Aside from a few disputes over territorial fishing waters, the kingdom that lay along the western shores of the lake and the Concord had been at peace for as long as Wind could remember. They had little reason to fight these days, not with the ever-present threat of the badgermen that infested the ruined city-swamp at the south end of the long lake.

"Where are their oarsmen?" Looking to the approaching ships dead ahead, Handy braced his upper arms on the gunwales to either side, while his lower hands he cupped over his eyes to block out the glare of the morning sun off the clouds overhead.

Wind kept propelling the canoe forward, but as he stroked through the water he studied the ships with greater care. The sails of all but one dropped as he watched, and he saw numerous anchors splash down into the freezing water. The biggest of the ships left the rest behind and proceeded toward the catamaran.

"What are they playing at?" Handy gave Wind a confused look.

"They mean to talk," Wind observed.

"An awfully big diplomatic mission, if you ask me." Handy's lower hands stroked the pommels of the long blades sheathed at his hips as they watched the great head of the wooden dragon slowly approach. Six great oars stabbed out into the lake and neatly backed water to bring the ship to a halt within easy calling distance.

When he saw a line of faces at the near rail of the ship, Handy sucked in a breath. "That's a lot of women and children."

"Halloo the ship!" The cry came from a red bearded man who stood at the neck of the dragon prow. The man waved at the *Little Abundance* with a wide brimmed leather hat and called out, "Parlay?"

"Permission to approach?" Wind called across the gap.

"Granted. With pleasure, and with a request that you relay our peaceable intent to your fleet."

Handy didn't move. Good man, Wind thought.

"We'll wait on that, thank you," Wind shouted back, his muscles already straining from the effort of closing the distance between the ships.

Ropes flung out from the near side of the dragon ship. Handy and Wind fastened them to their ship, and they were reeled in the last few yards. Handy stayed in the *Little Abundance*, and Wind stood up, gripped the gunwale of the dragon ship, and reached up and pulled himself aboard.

He was helped by the strong grip of the red-bearded man. Up close, Wind noted had the creased and sun-browned face of a man who spent his life on deep and dangerous waters. "Captain Ironmane, of his late majesty's fisheries, at your service, young man."

"Wind," he replied, shaking the man's calloused hand in a firm grip. "Duly designated envoy of," his voice caught as he glanced around the narrow deck of the ship. With effort he finished, "of the Concordat's local militia."

His attention had been stolen by the sorry state of the vessel. It was crowded with sad-faced women and teary-eyed children. He counted only six men of fighting age on a ship that could have held forty. All of the men, and several of the boys, bore the signs of struggle—bruises, and red-stained bandages wrapped around arms or legs, and in one case, covering an eye. Only the captain was uninjured. Sacks and boxes had been shoved everywhere with little thought or organization of the ship, or the contents. Chickens huddled out in the breeze, and a few miserable goats had been tied to the mast on short leads.

Captain Ironmane caught Wind's silent judgment of the sorry state of the ship and ruefully admitted, "Aye lad. We fled Racine. We are not here to fight or steal your waters or your fishing grounds. We are here to ask for refuge."

"Handy," Wind called out over the side of the dragon ship. "Run up the blue flag."

"It was the badgermen," the captain started to explain, but Wind held up the palm of one hand.

"I'm not the one you need to talk to," Wind explained. "I'm just here to find out whether you meant to fight or talk. You caught us off guard."

"Lot of that going around," the captain said.

"Strange days," Wind agreed.

"You haven't the slightest idea."

They waited for Twomind's arrival in silence, which gave Wind time to study the ship. He had never been aboard a Kingdom ship before, only met them on the water far from land to exchange rumors and a few small trade goods. The Kingdom made excellent cheeses and a rich beer, which they often traded for the sweet wines and spicy sausages Wind carried on every fishing trip for just such trades. But he had only ever seen the ships from his own small canoe, handing the goods up and over the rail.

With the practiced eye of a sailor, he saw that even with a wider beam, the ships were as crowded as their own. Extra space was taken up by twin ranks of rowing benches along either side. The square rigging was strange to his eyes, but he recognized a certain efficiency in the way they were laid out. The ship lost some maneuverability, but with the support of the oarsman, it could be lightning fast in short bursts. When he had seen enough, Wind turned his eye to the occupants.

Fearful faces eyed him with traces of hope that made him feel awkward. Most were still huddled in small groups and tucked into corners, their faces strained and weary. He saw mothers with arms around children. There were old men and women leaning against each other for physical and emotional comfort. Wind saw tear-streaked faces, smudged with dirt and ash.

The men stood about, jaws tight with pain and shame. They had taken a beating, but bore themselves with a steely resolve, as though they resented the need to look to the Concord for aid. Wind couldn't bear their stares, so he turned to watch the triangular sails of his countrymen approach. They stopped just out of bow shot. Wind thought they were perhaps waiting for the arrival of the fleet from South Haven.

"Fleet" was a pretty fancy word for the motley collection of independently-owned ships of the Concordat. They were built for fishing but manned by hardy souls fond of fighting on the open sea against terrible odds. Frequent raids by the swamp rats to the south swept the timid and unlucky from the decks on a regular basis.

Was that what this was about? Wind had no time to follow the thought. He cleared his throat and turned to Captain Ironmane. "As you are guests in our waters, the..."

He trailed off as the men of the ship tensed. Ironmane made a slight gesture and said, "We will conduct the meeting on your ships." To those around him he said in a louder voice, "As is customary. The Concordat will honor that tradition." He pointed to the man with a bloody bandage over one eye and said, "Popper, you have the helm until my return. Blackout will come with me."

An old woman whimpered as her man pried himself from her grip. He stood on unsteady legs, and one of his kin rushed to help him to the side of the ship. To Wind, he seemed an odd choice as a second. Usually the captains took their second in command, a fierce and intimidating warrior, or even a distinguished talker. The oldster could barely clamber over the rail and needed all four of Handy's arms to make it safely into the lower vessel.

The Captain provided no clue to his rationale during the short paddle back to the combined fleets of Wind's village and the Havenites, which waited together in a group two hundred yards north of the Racine fleet, flanking them lest the discussions lead to violence.

It took a little more effort to get the old man they called Blackout aboard the larger Pride of

Sparta. He bore the indignity of riding up into the ship on a plank lowered by rope with stoic grace but waved off any assistance and hobbled under his own power to where Captain Twomind and Ironmane had dispensed with the formalities. The ship's cook pressed warm mugs of tea into the hands of their guests. In the cold morning air, the light breeze felt like an arctic blast, and the warm tea reminded them of better summer days to come.

"The badgermen indeed," Captain Ironmane answered Twomind's discreet inquiry. "They came sweeping out of those blasted towers of theirs in numbers you can't imagine."

"Figured it wasn't another raid," Twomind mused. "That smoking iron monster of theirs wouldn't have let so many ships get away."

Ironmane shook his head, an action that sent his long red hair rippling against his chest. His face darkened. "If we could get our hands on a few rifles, figure out how they work, then we'd drive the critters off the lake once and for all."

"Dream big," Twomind replied. "You won't get rifles from the Technocracy. They only parcel them out to the badgermen to keep us in check. Unless you want to don the yoke of the Technocracy."

Ironmane spit on the deck. "Our king, God save him, would never submit to bureaucrats."

"Nor would our congress," Twomind agreed. "The Technocracy's subjects might be safe behind those magic weapons, but they bear a heavy cost. What is it?" Ironmane kept looking south, as though he expected something awful to appear on the horizon.

"We didn't see the black ship on our way here. I can almost hear it coming for us now."

"It's never sailed in winter before."

The Racine captain heaved a great sigh, his eyes haunted. "They've never launched an all-out war before, either."

"War?" Startled, the word leapt from Wind unbidden. Ironmane turned sad eyes toward Wind. "Aye. War. Thousands of them rode at us on those magnificent horses of theirs, a great black wave of them. Ripped through us like we weren't even there. Slaughtered us like cattle. All we could do was hold them off long enough to get to the ships. We bought the king some time and hugged the shore to make them think we were headed north, but when the sun went down, we could see fires all along the coast. Few could still fight." He hung his head in shame. "We ran for safety."

Twomind tilted his head to catch the Racine captain's eye. "To us?"

"Aye," Ironmane said, eyes still downcast. "What else could we do?"

The men gathered around them eyed each other, uncertain. Wind detected a pugnacious stubbornness in the old man's eyes, as though daring them to start a fight with him and sti-fled a grin of respect for the codger.

Twomind turned away from Ironmane. He gripped the wooden rail of his ship tight-ly with both hands and gazed out across the dark water. He seemed to study the sad fleet of dragon-prowed ships, silent and buried deep within his own thoughts. Wind had seen the man like this before every time he faced a difficult choice, which as the duly-elected leader of their village happened on a regular basis. Inside the man's head, two brains struggled to make sense of this changing world.

If the Kingdom fell, the badgermen would come for the Concordat next. No longer pinched between the men along either side of the long freshwater sea, their master could direct his full might against the Concordat. It would take time for them to secure their holdings, perhaps a year or so, but unless the Technocracy intervened, the end of that fight was a foregone conclusion. Congress could call up the militias. They would muster, meet the enemy, and fight, but all the talents of the New Men stood little chance of success in stemming the tide against which the Kingdom had failed.

The Maplemen of the north would be no help, either. Too slow and set in their soil, they cared little for the affairs of the hyperactive creatures scurrying about in the lands to their south.

The Concordat made for a slim hope of safety against such hate. The addition of a dozen ships from the Kingdom would help. If the men aboard possessed the right talents, it might tip the balance in their favor.

Wind first looked to Handy, a formidable foe with his three flashing blades coming at

you from behind the shield he carried in his fourth hand. He had a way of disguising which hand held the shield that complicated fights against him.

Wind then looked to the old man, and a faint understanding dawned. Whatever that man's talent, it had to be formidable, because it seemed to him that Ironmane felt it protected him against every man on board the *Spirit of Sparta*.

"Okay," Twomind decided, disturbing Wind's reverie. "Understand, whatever we decide here will have to be approved by Congress, but we can allay their fears with a few simple precautions."

Ironmane had looked up from the deck, hope shining in his eyes until he heard the last word. "Precautions?"

"What do you think will happen," Twomind crossed his arms and leaned back against the rail.

Suspicious, the Racine man slowly explained, "The ruins along Saint Claire have never been cleared, even after all these years. We can sail around the peninsula and make a new home there. We will appoint a king to serve in your congress. You gain strong backs, cleared ground, and a trustworthy buffer against the Technocracy."

"You aim to establish a new kingdom in our lands."

"No," Ironmane protested. "We aim to swear fealty to your congress. We only ask that you allow us to live according to our customs. Which," he hastened to add, "we will adapt to accommodate your less, uh, meritorious ways."

Twomind stared back. "As I thought," he said dispassionately, "You don't want to become members of the Concordat. You want to be men of the king, living in the Concordat's borders." He shook his head. "No chance. Your people can join ours, but we will not accept a community of monarchists within our republic. If you want succor, then your ships will be distributed, one to each town or village along our coast. One man to claim each ship as his rightful possession can remain. Families without a ship must be settled inland, one per town. Perhaps two in the larger cities of the Concordat."

Ironmane's mood darkened as the conditions were listed. He considered for a moment, then growled, "Scattered to the wind, our children will grow up with little understanding of who they are."

"No," Twomind countered with iron in his voice, "They will grow up as members of the Concord." His voice softened as he added, "But at least they will grow up."

"You would destroy my people."

"The badgermen have already destroyed them. The Concordat offers them a chance to remain alive. If that doesn't suit them, you can sail back to your king."

"My king is dead."

"Your people don't have to be."

Ironmane looked to his second. Wind followed his gaze and found the old man standing tall and proud, his hands balled up into fists. A tense feeling gathered in the air, like the pressure just before a storm burst upon the land. Everything hung in the balance and Wind realized he wasn't the only one to feel it. Every man around him was tense with anticipation. All looked to Ironmane.

Finally, after what felt like an age, the red-bearded captain sighed, "I am sorry, my father."

The old man nodded, and the pressure released, slow and easy.

Wind could breathe again. He didn't realize he had been holding his breath until the old man let go his fists and slumped back down to his usual posture.

"You have a deal," Ironmane sighed. "I ask that you permit my own family to settle in your village." His brows knit with a barely concealed wrath. "I'd like to be close enough to the swamp to raid the badgermen."

Twomind shrugged. "Up to the Congress, but I'll argue for it. Wherever you dock your ship, it will be your ship from here on out. Leave Concord ships alone, and you can go a-pirate to your heart's content."

Ironmane showed his teeth in a feral grin. "That's right," he said slowly. "I can. I don't have to ask the king's permission."

"There," Twomind smiled and offered his hand to Ironmane. "You see? A silver lining. Although, in this case the cloud you're looking behind is your decision to save all of those lives." He waved to the blue and white sails of the captain's refugee fleet. "While the Concord stands unbroken, hope remains."

"Ship ahoy!"

Every man aboard looked up to the tip of the mast overhead, where Spider clung, bare-handed and barefoot. One of his fat fingers pointed southwest, and the men on the deck all surged for the port rail, eyes straining to catch sight of the approaching sail. Instead they found a small black stain rising on the horizon.

"The black ship!" half a dozen voices cried.

"Get me back to my ship," Ironmane moaned, his ruddy face drained of color.

That signal sent men racing in every direction.

Twomind shouted orders into the chaos around them, sparing only a nod to send Wind back to the *Little Abundance*. They hustled Ironmane and Blackout back into the outrigger canoe and shoved away from the larger ship. "They've really stuck their muzzle in it this time, boys!" Then, louder, "Ironmane, get your people repositioned. We're going after it! Give me three good ships full of men, and together we can sink that bastard!"

"Are you mad?" Ironmane stood and shouted back to the *Spirit of Sparta*. His sea legs and practiced balance barely disturbed the small craft as Handy drove them forward under oar power and Wind rushed to set the sail. "That thing is powered by the fires of hell! Steel skin and a cannon that could sink us all in a single shot!"

Twomind answered, "We outnumber that

ship twenty-seven to one. Thirty with your ships. I thought the men of Racine were stalwart. This is your chance at redemption. One last blow against the creatures that destroyed your kingdom and killed your monarch. Come on, man!"

Ironmane threw his head back, the light breeze ruffling his long fiery locks of hair and laughed loud and hard. "You easterners are a stubborn lot. You'll have your three ships. And a little something extra besides." He turned and dropped back into the canoe with a thump, then leaned forward, his hands on Blackout's shoulders. "What do you say, father? One more adventure?"

The old man threw up one hand that conveyed a mix of irritation and consent all at once. Ironmane laughed, but he could not take his eyes off that black smudge on the horizon.

When they reached the Racine ships, Ironmane didn't rise from his seat. He sat and stroked his beard as he studied the horizon to the southwest.

"Captain," Handy said when he noticed the redhead's reticence. "Captain Ironmane, I mean. Are you...?" He waved up at the hands reaching down to them. Ironmane heaved his heavy frame around in his seat, his eyes afire with intense passion. "Is it true? A captain of the Concordat can sail his ship as he sees fit?"

"Uh," Wind was taken aback. He thought that's how all ships worked. "Sure, I guess. I mean, yeah."

"And you are the captain of this ship?" Ironmane bounced a fist against the rail of the *Little Abundance*.

"Yes." Wind said slowly, uncertain of where the man's questions were leading him.

"And you want to sink that black ship once and for all."

Irritated at the man's circuitous questions, Wind wiped the confusion from his face and demanded, "What are you getting at, Captain?"

"We turn that ship into a sitting duck. Easy pickings for the fleet. But trust me."

Handy watched the plea from his seat at the prow. One eyebrow was cocked high with curiosity.

The old man sat huddled just ahead of Ironmane. Implacable.

"How?" Wind asked.

"Explanations have to wait until we are on our way. We have to beat the rest of this fleet to the black ship if we have a chance of success. Can you do it? Will you take us to that ship?"

Wind only needed a moment to consider. Ironmane had been through a long night. He should have feared the black ship. He had guided the remnants of his own village out of the jaws of death and into the safety of the Concordat. He thought of Abundance at home, by now likely feeding the little ones a hot oat breakfast, all the while worried sick. If there was even a chance that they could end the threat of the ship appearing in the middle of the night and carrying off his beloved wife or burning his home to the ground, Wind knew he could not turn down the offer.

Besides all that, Wind had dreamed of the day he could stop carrying great tidings about the lake and perhaps be the cause of them. This could be his only chance.

"Yes. We can pretend to request parlay," he suggested. At the very least, they might delay the black ship long enough for Twomind to improve whatever plan he had up his sleeve, if nothing else.

No sooner had he agreed than Handy hissed, "Are you serious? You want to fight the black ship? The four of us? In a canoe?"

Something about the way Blackout just sat there, huddled for warmth against the winter breeze, told Wind that Ironmane knew what he was doing. Ironmane was smart enough to accept Twomind's conditions, even when he didn't know the man's talent.

Twomind had great bulging temples that suggested a quick wit, but there were a lot of New Men around with that look who fared much worse in the talent lottery. Most died at birth, but Wind had heard of one wanderer whose wide forehead danced with shadowy images of whatever was on his mind at the time. That one made a good living as a walking showman, doing voices for the characters he imagined. According to the stories, he wore a large hat when not performing, lest his talent betray his daily thoughts. If your forehead shows what you're thinking, you've got to wear a hat, Wind reasoned. He hoped to see the man perform one day.

While Wind reflected on the strange twists of fate and the atom that had gifted the men of the Concord with unpredictable talents, Ironmane was busy shouting orders at Popper. The acting captain leaned over the rail, comfortable with his new command, and sent down a shield and small oar for Ironmane's use.

Then they were off, four oars in the water, and the sail trimmed just right. They zipped along at a good clip, tacked when they neared the shore, and raced back out into the wide-open waters of the lake.

"A good little ship," Ironmane said over his shoulder once they put a couple of miles between them and the assembling fleet. Tired from the effort of rowing, he pulled his oar from the water to catch his breath. "What's her name?"

"Little Abundance," Wind answered easily enough. "After my wife."

"An interesting name."

"He," Handy puffed, "Has. Six. Kids."

"So far," Wind laughed, his arms still pumping. "Take a break before you kill yourself."

Ironmane slid the oar into the space under his narrow seat and rubbed his shoulders to work out knots that had formed during the sprint from the fleet. "What's your secret?" Ironmane asked, clearly curious about Wind's incredible stamina.

It was a strange question. Among new men, it was not a subject discussed in polite company. The physical signs of a talent, and the name bestowed by the local priest on a boy or girl's coming-of-age ceremony, were usually enough to deduce how the atom had affected one. When they weren't, it was left to the man or woman to reveal their talents in their own good time.

Wind longed to ask about Blackout's gift, but he held his tongue. Instead, he ignored the breach of conduct and tapped his chest. "Extra lung. Extra heart." He tapped the polished wooden bench between his legs. "Lots of time spent sitting right here developing them. Now it's your turn. Do you have something to tell me? Something about how four men in an outrigger are going to stop the black ship when dozens of larger ships have sunk beneath its cannons?"

Ironmane held up one finger in a silent gesture of "Just you wait." He drew his sword, a curious leaf-bladed affair longer than Wind and Handy's. Elegant, but no less deadly than their more utilitarian short, straight blades. He shrugged out of his jacket, then pulled off his wool sweater and his white undershirt, exposing his hirsute chest, arms, and back to the frigid air. Beneath the natural covering of short auburn hair, Wind counted three large purple bruises ringed with halos of yellow.

Wind leaned to one side, his oar still marking time. "Handy, are you watching this?"

Handy turned around in time to see Ironmane place one sharp edge of his blade against his forearm and drag it hard in a sweeping arc through his flesh. Handy started, but Wind had guessed the man's talent before the blade scraped harmlessly over his arm.

"Shanks of steel," Wind deduced. "Impressive. Explains why you are the only one of your men to escape unhurt."

Ironmane chuckled and explained, "Not unhurt, just uncut. The impact of one of those slug throwers of theirs might not tear my flesh thanks my talent, but it still feels like the kick of a mule. I've bruises to spare."

"Explains the long hair and beard," Handy pointed out from the prow.

Ironmane laughed openly at that observation. "That and it makes me look dashing, or so the missus says." His face fell when he said that. A haunted look past over his face, a look he hid by struggling back into his undershirt and long leather jacket.

"Last night?" Wind asked.

"Aye," Blackout answered when his son did not. "She had a way with flames, my little Blaze did. Saw her little ones safe aboard ship, and then walked back into Racine to lay down a ring that the swamp rats could not cross."

"She saved us all," Ironmane murmured.

"She saved us all," Blackout nodded.

"And now she shall be avenged," Wind said, hoping his voice carried more conviction than he felt.

They sailed in silence for a time. Before long Wind had to pause to remove his woolen cap and loosen his fur-lined coat. He might not tire, but his exertions warmed him, and he began to sweat despite the cold and wind. Tonight, if he survived, he would be ravenous and ready for a feast to replenish the energy spent over this marathon session on the water.

Away to the east, the morning sun, hidden behind thick clouds that trapped its heat, had likely burned off the snow that dusted the land.

Ahead, the low smudge had grown to a towering column of dark smoke that poured from the top of two tall stacks set to either side of the black ship. It looked like a toy on the horizon, but Wind could picture the details of the vile thing in his mind. Dark metal with an underslung prow with which it rammed ships. The wide beam of the black ship and the curve of that terrible ram flung its enemies in either direction as its mechanical drives, coal eaters that fed great wheels at the center of either rail of the ship, propelled the ship inexorably forward. Nothing short of mother earth or towering waves could stop that black engine of death. They were headed straight for it. The men took a moment to tack a few points into the breeze. Wind looked north and saw the sails of the combined Kingdom and Concordat fleet, the largest accumulation he had ever seen, matching their course. Every sailor and fisherman on every ship knew that the black ship paid little heed to wind or current, and even ignored the threat of kelp sharks and gillmen. They did not have the luxury of coal-fired engines and so sought to come upon their prey as fast as possible from upwind.

"We don't really have much room left," Handy pointed out from the front of the little boat. "If you have a plan, now would be a good time."

"I have to agree, Captain," Wind added. "I'd put your hide, Handy's extra arms, and my disregard for weariness up against any five of those rifle-toting swamp rats. But that," he gestured with his oar. "That's something else entirely."

"Better tell 'em," the old man grunted.

"My father-in-law," Ironmane explained. "We need to get him inside the decks of that ship."

"Why?" Wind asked. "What could he do?"

"They don't call me Blackout because I make men drunk," the old man answered cryptically.

"You men of the Kingdom love your secrets, don't you?" Handy had had enough. "Speak plain. What do we do if they let us aboard that ship?"

"Get my father-in-law below decks. With his talent, he can put every creature aboard out of action for an hour. But he has to get below-decks, into her guts. He can't do it through steel plating."

Wind put up his oar. "This is madness. Even if we avoided those fat cannons, we four couldn't board that monster and then fight our way below."

"We won't have to," Ironmane answered. "Not if we ask for a parlay."

Wind sneered, "Betray the peace of parlay?"

Ironmane turned in his seat. "We betray parlay. Yes. Men have honored that tradition from time immemorial. From before the birth of the atom and breaking of the world. It is sacrosanct and inviolable. Not just for we men of the lake shores, but for the men of the Technocracy as well." He pointed at the looming prow of the metal monster bearing down upon them. "They walk as men, but act as beasts. They honor nothing and hold nothing sacrosanct. Those are not men."

"Can't break an agreement with critters that never agreed," Blackout added.

"You cut to the heart of things, old man," Wind said. He set his oar aside and raised the white flag of truce. "All right. I don't like it, but," he looked over his shoulder to the approaching fleet of fragile wooden vessels, "I like them more than I dislike your plan."

Oar back in the water, Wind again prodded Ironmane. "The plan?"

The sound of the black ship's engines had grown, and now was joined by a raucous jeering. Dark, long faces lined the rail along a high forecastle set just aft of the ram carving a white spume through the cold water of the lake. Two high chimneys belched black clouds into the air behind that, and then a low waist gave way to twin half-circles, one to each flank, near the stern. The dark sides of the hull glinted dull gray in the overcast light, scales of metal like those of a fish, all pointing toward the stern.

It flew no flag, needing none, and not caring to communicate with the fragile men who trespassed upon the long and wide lake that they claimed as their own.

The white spray at the ram died, and to the dismay of the men aboard the *Little Abundance*, the ship turned in place. A white column of smoke billowed out from black squares in her flank, followed by a dull boom, then a geyser of water spewed up from the surface of the lake just ahead of their outrigger canoe.

A warning shot.

Wind's hearts stalled within his chest. For a moment he longed once more to trail after the fighting ships, to carry word of this black monster rather than face it in his tiny lake-bound vessel. Then anger welled up in his heart as the echo of the cannon shot faded, only to be replaced by the hooting laughter of the things on board the black ship. The figures lining the rail of the forecastle resolved into hooting and waving creatures out of nightmare. The whole ship grew larger. Ugly faces, sharp-eared and beady-eyed, with protruding white muzzles filled with little pointed teeth and long pink tongues that lolled when they threw back their heads and chortled. They wore nothing but black pants and heavy boots, distinct against the dark gray fur that covered their exposed torsos and protected them from the winter air. Glints of bright gold shone in their tufted ears and jowly faces, piercings that provided the only spark of color on the black ship.

He had never seen them so clearly before. Both his previous sightings occurred on dark summer nights by the flickering blaze of roofs ignited by the raiding parties. They looked no less menacing by the light of the cold winter sun. These were not men. They were animals, wild and savage, and Wind knew Ironmane was right. After generations of swift and cowardly night attacks on his people, Wind owed the howling things no respect, no assurances, and no honorable conduct.

That they had not been blasted out of the water already might be considered a good sign. Wind bided his time, backing water to keep them at a distance from the larger ship. He donned his thick wool cap and shrugged into his heavy coat. The fur and leather trapped the heat of his exertions but might provide some protection against the things on that ship when the fighting started.

The lines of the raiding ship mimicked those of the wooden ships men used to cross and fish the lake, but the sharp angles and blocky mass of the ironclad lent it an air of cold and calculating animosity. Wind's little catamaran sat upwind of the black ship. The breeze carried the twin plumes of the hellish smoke that poured from the ironclad's stacks away from the *Little Abundance*.

Ironmane muttered under his breath, then bellowed. "Halloo the ship!"

At the rail, the largest of the creatures stood shirtless in the same dark pants and boots, but its forearms were encased in burnished steel, and its long, tapered head encased in a matching helmet. Unlike the dark gray fur of his compatriots, his was black as pitch.

The big one waited a moment, then shrugged one shoulder and slid a long weapon from its back. It held a wooden stock to shoulder and directed a sleeve of metal their way. It looked down a small spyglass set atop the firearm, and the sharp crack of the shot hit them at the same instant splinters flew from the mast a few inches over Wind's head. Instinctively, the men in the little catamaran ducked.

"Your lives belong to me," the badgerman growled. The head badgerman lowered its weapon slowly amid howls of triumph from its crew. Then it summoned them to approach by beckoning with one large, claw tipped paw.

As they paddled closer, the leader roared. "You bring tribute?" Its tight jowls and long, thin tongue lent a sloppiness to its speech.

Wind could not tell if it was a question or a command, nor did he care. Either way, it betrayed the thing's desire, a desire Wind could use as leverage. "Yes!" Wind shouted. "Slaves for tribute! We are the heralds of the fleet!"

The beastman licked his chops and imperiously waved them forward.

The *Little Abundance* rowed and moments later their ship struck the ironclad with a dull thump, and Handy caught the two lines tossed their way, which he expertly used to tie up to the steel ship. They scrambled up a set of rungs fastened onto her hull and up onto the deck. To Wind's surprise, Blackout sprang up the ladder without hesitation, leading him to wonder if the old man's earlier frailty and need for assistance in getting on the Spirit of Sparta had been a clever ruse or a mischievous prank.

Their hosts looked even more bestial up close. Arrogant and dismissive, they watched as the four men clambered up the inclined steel of the ironclad and over the solid gunwale to stand on the heavy wood planks of the deck. There, the badgermen hissed and jostled and pawed at them.

Wind smelled the rank odor of their sweat and musk. He gritted his teeth at the leathery feel of the pads on their paws and bore the handling with stoic determination until finally the big badgerman roared. Then the things fell back, one ripping away Wind's bow as it retreated to its mates.

The big badgerman watched the abuse from atop the forecastle, at the top of a steep flight of steps flanked by doors down into the depths of the ship. It stood with hands on hips and feet spread wide. It had slung the long weapon back over its shoulder, but Wind could see that the top of the device had been fitted with a bayonet.

They stood three ranks deep, with several more at the rail that protected sailors on the forecastle from a fall down to the main deck. Wind saw no easy or safe access for Blackout to go below. He realized they'd have to fight their way through twenty of the well-armed badgermen.

The leader held out a large paw. "Give now!" Its leader's voice echoed, made resonant and distant by the helmet it wore.

Wind spread his hands and bowed low. "Oh, great and terrible masters of the lake, we have heard of the justice your lord meted out to the men of the west. Fearful neighbors are we, and when three ships fled to us seeking escape from your wise and judicious reckoning, we captured them. Even now my fellow captains bring them your way." Wind pointed north and a little west, where the blue and white squares sailed, intermingled with the red triangles of the Concordat fleet.

The thing in the burnished steel mask crossed its thick arms over its powerful chest and lifted its armored chin in a sharp gesture that meant nothing to Wind.

It spoke. "Why come you first?"

Wind's voice caught as the answer seemed obvious to him. He was a messenger. He flew the white flag of truce. Why else would he come?

"Great and powerful master," Ironmane broke in, sensing Wind's discomfiture. He also bowed low, hands spread wide. His voice sounded high and meek, a startling change from the gravel and weight it normally possessed. "We hastened to bring you the news so that you might spare our ships from your wrath."

Again, the thing jerked its chin upward. "Yes," it crooned. "Your ships are nothing. Sticks on the waves compared to mine. Return to your fleet. Tell them to place the slaves on dragon ships and depart."

"Master," Ironmane stood, hands raised in supplication. Hastily, he added. "We have been instructed to beg of you. In your mercy, with this tribute of slaves, we beseech you not raid upon our shores in the coming year."

The request hung in the air for a moment. Every badgerman froze in surprise at the affront of a mere man making demands to the master of the lake. A snort echoed out from the helmet, quickly followed by a raucous chorus of guffaws from the assembled crowd. The thick-waisted man-things threw their heads back, and slapped each other on the back, and turned to eye each other with mirth. That left them unprepared for Handy's whirling blades.

Handy had stood back, sheltered behind the broad back of Ironmane with his head hung low in feigned fear and shame. On edge and unable to wait for the perfect moment, he seized the first sign of distraction to draw the four blades at his belt and shoulder his way between the two captains. He howled like a banshee and threw himself with wild abandon at the massed group of animal men. Pressed against each other, and utterly certain of their technological superiority, the badgermen wasted precious moments processing the suicidal attack, and then struggled to remove the long rifles from their backs. Those that held them in hand strained to bring them to bear, but found their efforts confounded by the close quarters of their mates and the sudden onslaught of flashing blades that cut into them.

Ironmane threw himself in front of the few badger-faced men who managed to bring weapons to shoulders. Wind heard the thunder and felt the hellish heat of those weapons, but Ironmane had thrown himself at them. Instinctively, they had fired on the immediate threat of the red-headed man, and they shrank back as the demon man-thing howled in pain and anger but did not check his reckless charge.

Wind stepped forward to guard Handy's exposed back and hacked about him with his blade. He spared no thought for anything save his strokes, that they land amid the black and white faces that surrounded he and his friend. Only Blackout stood his ground amidships, useless until the strength of the younger men cleared a path for him to the hatch.

Wind's vision shrank to a narrow tunnel filled with sweeping blades, snarling muzzles, and ripping claws. At the same time, his sense of the self expanded, his hair stood on end, and he became hyper-aware of the heat of bodies around him. His hearts thundered in his chest. Lines of red etched across his shoulder and he felt his heavy coat ripped to shreds as a claw slipped past his frantic guard. His blade cut through dark fur and flesh. Hot blood splashed across his face, and he spat in disgust.

With the enemy's attention occupied by Handy's whirlwind of death and the impervious red demon Ironmane, the old man made himself small and began to edge along the port gunwale.

The leader of the beasts, made furious by the havoc on his main deck, began barking orders at the beastmen around him. The stairs down to the main deck blocked, he ordered them to raise their weapons to shoulders and aim into the fray. At a command, they fired as one.

The cannonade of gunfire nearly deafened Wind. White sulfurous smoke filled the air and clouded his vision. He screamed and threw himself toward the knot of warriors, but pulled back when a line of steel points, blades affixed to the fronts of their weapons, appeared through the haze. He turned to retreat, and a leather-clad figure tumbled across his path.

Handy.

His oldest friend crashed down to the deck, skidded on the blood-slicked surface, and lay still. One lower left arm lay bent at an unnatural angle, and a weeping wound in his upper right shoulder added more crimson to the smears on the deck.

Wind looked up and found himself face to face with the leader of the badgermen. The large black figure strode through the lingering haze of sulfurous smoke, barrel and blade of his weapon leading the way.

"Blackout!" Wind wailed as he steeled him-self to face the monster. He held his sword in a low two-handed grip and braced his legs wide.

"Hold fast!" Ironmane shouted across the din.

Wind had lost all sense of direction. He could not tell from whence Ironmane's voice had come, and he had no time to think. The great badgerman's finger tightened, and Wind dove to the side as thunder sounded in his ears and something snapped past his head with a vicious buzz. Before Wind could get his feet back under him the leader's blade thrust at him and Wind rolled to escape. But he could not avoid a heavy kick that struck his chest and drove the air from his center lung.

He lashed out with his blade, a feeble blow that caught a calf muscle and brought down a badgerman who clutched the wound and screamed in pain. Something smashed his sword hand and hammered it against the deck. White pain consumed him. His hand went limp and useless, and Wind watched in horror as his blade was kicked away.

Paws snatched at his leather coat and his wrists and dragged him across the deck. Oth-ers struck at him, fists and feet and claws smashed and tore at him, bathing his body in pain. He curled into position he did not long hold as the feral beast men clambered over each other in their bloodlust.

Wind had a momentary glimpse through a forest of black legs. Ironmane crouched near the hatch, blows raining down upon him as he knelt on one knee, pressed one splayed hand to the deck, and tried to stand amid a cluster of falling, smashing, cutting clawed hands.

Behind him, Blackout stood half inside the open hatch.

He hung there, his body leaning inside the dim confines of the ship, impaled on one of the spiked tip of a weapon. His hands were limp at his sides.

Wind's hearts broke. Despair washed over him, followed by a strange, energizing sensation that filled the air around him. It assaulted some nameless sense that was not quite touch and not quite hearing. The same sense that Empath tapped into when he sent a message through the ether.

A profound hopelessness crashed over Wind like an avalanche. So great was this renewed despair that it sucked the air out of his lungs and stilled his hearts. Tears filled his eyes. In his sorrow and shock, he did not hear the badgermen that held him tumble and clatter to the deck, nor did he realize they had let go of his body until his hands instinctively reached out to stop his fall.

The crushed bones and tendons of his hand struck the deck and sent a shockwave of agony through him that nearly caused him to lose consciousness. He lay still, his head filled with a strange sound. A steady rhythm of two beats, soft then hard. Soft, then hard. An odd sound. Like that of Abundance when he lay his head on her chest. Nothing like his own heartbeat, which sounded with a militaristic four beat. Three soft taps then a thump.

Da da da DUM, da da da DUM.

Strange days.

His head wasn't lying in Abundance's lap. It lay on cold, hard wood.

He gasped. Fought to fill his emptied lungs. His eyes snapped open and he cast about the deck of the ship, memories of blood and screams and stabbing bolts of fire and buzzing death inches away from his ear.

He rolled to his back, breathed hard, and looked about.

The old man had done it. Not a single creature stood.

Wind heaved himself to his belly, and then shoved himself to his knees, straightened, and found himself alone among the living. Still cradling his hand, he rose to a half-crouch and shoved his body upright.

It took a moment before the wave of vertigo passed. The small Concordat fleet with its Kingdom auxiliary raced toward him, white spray flickering against their prows and colorful sails filled with the fresh morning breeze.

Something rumbled beneath his feet and fresh black smoke poured anew from the stacks overhead. As Wind watched, Blackout's body began sliding into the depths of the black ship. A fur covered arm held the hatch open.

No—not open. The arm belonged to a badgerman, but he was trying to pull the hatch shut. He would have done so already had Blackout's still body not fallen over the lower ledge of the portal.

The badgerman saw Wind and snarled but did not halt in his efforts to close the hatch.

Wind ripped one of the strange rifles from the dead hand of a fallen badgerman. He held it awkwardly and lay the barrel over his right forearm. He pulled the trigger as he had seen the others do, and the device punched him in the shoulder so hard he dropped it. But the thunder sounded, the flame stabbed, and the breeze carried away the white smoke.

The badgerman was gone.

The hatch lay nearly shut, the toes of Blackout's boots still holding it open.

Wind lunged to prevent the door from closing completely. He feared that his wild shot had scared the badgerman, that he would return in seconds to lock the hatch. He stumbled over a fallen creature, who let out a groan and rolled over onto its belly, head cradled in the crook of one arm.

The fallen weren't dead. Only unconscious, but Wind's clumsy haste had woken the badgerman at his feet. Perhaps hope remained for Handy and Ironmane!

Wind found Handy's fallen body and shook it to no avail. The man had suffered terrible wounds and had given up his life for the chance of ending this terrible ship's hold on his people.

Wind snatched up one of Handy's blades. The pain in his broken right hand receded, washed away by adrenaline and a righteous wrath that filled him at the sight of his friend broken and discarded on the deck of the black ship.

He strode toward the hatch, pried it open with the heel of his boot, and descended into the dark, cacophonous hell that lay in the belly of the beast.

A howling creature rushed him, a wrench held high in its fist. It died with a whimper against the faster blade which found its belly.

Heat washed over Wind, and brimstone filled his lungs. His world shrank down to a gloomy, narrow passage walled in with tubes of metal, lit by flickering orange and blood red. They died as quickly as they came at him.

He leapt upon a large cylinder set upon a wooden carriage with tiny wooden wheels. He kicked a beast in the teeth, cut another one across the face. They cowered before his steady assault.

There was no more Wind. The man that strode through the narrow passages of the black ship was a cold and resolute force of nature, doom made manifest, and as implacable as death.

The combined weight of generations of bitter loss drove him forward. The screams of countless women dragged aboard this monstrous warship wailed in his heart, a demonic choir that propelled him onward and gave wings to his short blade. The everyday strain, the constant nervous pull of the lake over the shoulders of men as they watched and prayed the black ship would pass them by, the shame of hoping that this doom would fall on another town, another ship, even that of a friend or ally rather than a man's own kin. All of it poured down through the ages and animated the shell that was once Wind with the cold rage of a righteous wrath that would not be denied on this day.

Flame speared at him, the white sulfurous smoke filled the bowels of the mechanical monster. Twice he felt the sting of the things. Once in his shoulder, and once in his thigh. His relentless march through the ship did not stop until the red blood of his enemies adorned every bulkhead and painted every floor.

The air grew hot and close, and his sense of direction failed him. This cold killing machine cared nothing for the wonders of the ship that surrounded him. It only thirsted for the death of his foes. He only longed to deliver the pent-up justice that these caricatures of men, ugly in form and spirit, had earned during generations of marauding and conquest.

The long passage on the lake. The hammer blow of Blackout's strange gift that felled the warriors on deck. The death march through the belly of the black ship. All of it finally overwhelmed him, and he staggered to one knee. With no more enemies to feed his fury, Wind finally fell.

He sat and listened in silence as the steady beat of their boots and awed shouts echoed on the planks above. He heard the creak of the hatch hinges as they descended belowdecks.

Ironmane himself, woken by the newly-arrived men of the fleet, led the party that combed the confines of the ship Wind had turned into a floating abattoir.

They found him sitting amid the carnage and ruin. The far-off stare in Wind's eyes, the extraordinary amount of blood covering his body, and the savage wounds that wept in his arm and leg gave them pause.

"Strange days," Wind muttered, too faint for them to make out the words.

Slowly, cautiously, Ironmane approached Wind. He crouched and held out one hand and called out Wind's name. "Are you okay, son?"

Wind answered, his voice far away and faint. "Our winter is ended. The world has been made anew."

And he closed his eyes.

A gentle rocking woke him.

A soft smile crossed his lips at the sensation of being on the lake, lulled by the motion of the waves. He heard the crunch and slog of boots somewhere close by and the world tilted beneath him. He was on his back and his head rose steeply above his boots.

He opened his eyes and squinted against the harsh glare of an overcast day. Beneath him, and growing farther away with every passing step, he saw the *Little Abundance* tied to the steel pilings that held back the earthen quay. The river was filled with the usual assortment of village boats, and two strange ships: a square-rigged dragon ship with rolled sails of blue and white, and a dark hulking monstrosity.

His body rocked, and his world jerked and pain flared up as wounds in his hand, arm, leg, and shoulder all vied for his attention. His head felt stuffed with wool. It took far too long to process the apology muttered by one of the men that carried his litter up the stone steps to the village. He waved indolently.

It was all right. He felt bad for making them carry him up the steps. He was Wind. The priest had christened him as such because he could run like his namesake. He shouldn't be carried. He tried to rise, but a firm hand on his unhurt shoulder pushed him down.

"You've done enough, son."

Wind canted his head to the side and gazed up past a thick belly and bright red beard to meet the gaze of Ironmane. The old captain's eyes were rimmed red and his lips were tight.

"I'm sorry for everything you've lost," whispered Wind.

Ironmane shook his head, a curt acknowledgment. "Not everything. Still got my boys. And a future."

They reached the top of the steps and Wind's litter leveled out. Above, the high steeple of the village church passed them by. A man leaned out, Empath, and waved.

Well done, echoed in Wind's head, and he returned the wave.

"And a bright new future it is, too," Ironmane added

"Oh?"

"While you were being tended, Twomind
turned the black ship over to me."

"You'll steer her through whatever shoals
come your way."

Ironmane smiled, tight-lipped. "I'll steer her
north and let the craftsmen up in Muskegon
take a crack at unraveling her secrets."

Wind returned the smile. "You're not going
to settle down," he accused his new friend.
"You're going to hole up in that fort and sneak
out to wreak vengeance on the swamp rats."

Ironmane chuckled, more of a feral growl of
anticipation than a mirthful laugh. "Come the
fall, they'll have many a sleepless winter night."

They had reached Wind's humble cabin.

Wind reached out to Ironmane. He blinked moisture from his eyes and murmured, "Help me up."

Ironmane paused, one foot on the bottom-
most stair that led up to Wind's wide porch.
He ordered the sailors carrying the litter to set
him down. He heaved Wind to his feet, and
after a deep breath his new friend could stand
on his own.

"I have a promise to keep, but first tell me
of Handy," Wind said.

Ironmane met Wind's look with open sorrow.
"His sacrifice will be remembered. The ironclad
will be rechristened *Four Hands of Vengeance*
come Sunday." Pride, sorrow, and regret all piled
on them until the throbbing pain in Wind's leg

grew too much to bear. He released Ironmane, but stumbled on the first step.

Ironmane caught him, guided him back to the steps, and then retreated a respectful distance once Wind reached the front door. In his years, the captain had learned to recognize when a man needed to stand on his own, and he would not intrude on a reunion such as this for all the ironclads in the world.

He stood with one hand on the door jamb and steeled himself for the onslaught of children about to crash into him. One last deep breath, and he yanked the door open.

The tide of children swelled the moment he stepped inside. Before he could warn them to be careful, his eyes met Abundance.

She stood at the sink, a rag and a plate in hand. "You came back," she said. Her eyes the color of a summer sky blinked back tears of profound relief.

"I tried," he replied.

And then the tide of small hugs, tender kisses, and questions about his adventure and pirates washed over him.

SYMBIOT

Jeffro Johnson

A long time ago in an America that doesn't exist anymore, fantasy role-playing games became a modest sensation. Book stores at nearly every small-town mall carried the imposing tomes of first edition *Advanced Dungeons & Dragons*. The red box Basic D&D set was already ubiquitous, available at Toys "R" Us at a price point well in reach of any young man capable of mowing a lawn. There was a D&D Saturday morning cartoon with its requisite toy line. A plethora of *Choose Your Own Adventure*-style game book lines as well, that often included stripped-down role-playing game rules of their own. No matter your age or level of sophistication, there was some sort of fantasy gaming product for you to sink your teeth into.

So many people were intrigued by these games at this time. You'd see them invoked in everything from block bustermovies to after-school specials. It was easy to get a game together. There were so many players. The hysteria of the D&D panic of the time even added intrigue which made them seem cooler than they were, maybe even a little dangerous.

Urban legends about the D&D scene's dark side were so compelling many parents simply forbade their children from playing at all. Fortunately, D&D's creators had an alternative already on the market: an offbeat science-fantasy game which not only defied most genre conventions, but one so strange that no one could ever conceivably confuse it with D&D: no spell-casting, wizardry, or demonic entities were included in the box. *Gamma World* was the hottest hot mess in tabletop gaming.

My edition features the iconic Larry Elmore cover depicting a man in powered armor brandishing a laser rifle while riding on the back of a giant mutant cyborg wolverine. A rugged mountain skyline serves as the backdrop. Every detail of the weaponry and the creature is painstakingly depicted. Both the animal's biology and the weapon s technology seem hyper-real. It is awesome. Inspiring, even—giving the impression that this would naturally be the *Heavy Metal* of role-playing games. As much as I love it, I have to admit the game inside was basically nothing like that.

Veteran role-players would of course recognize the six player-character attributes identical to those from the original *Dungeons & Dragons* game—the sole exception being the Wisdom stat changed to Mental Strength. (This is a game where psionic ability is more important than a mastery of the proverbs of Solomon.) And being set in an impossible post-apocalyptic future, the concept of alignment was excised from the rules as well. This would not be a game of cosmic conflict waged between the forces of Law and Chaos; instead, it was all about benighted mutants crawling out of the wastes of a bizarre post-apocalyptic wasteland of death and radiation.

Hardy souls that they were, a single die roll for hit points was an insufficient measure of a character's fortitude. *Gamma World* grants you a number of six-sided dice equal to your constitution score and even applies further bonuses. Starting characters could easily be tougher than late-career D&D characters. For players suffering from a thousand-yard stare after losing countless first-level fighters to arbitrary falls into pit traps, rat bite, and other ludicrously unheroic fates, this would have seemed a godsend. But those massive quantities of hit points came with a catch: the new game's setting was exponentially more dangerous and violent than the typical town-and-dungeon scenario that starting D&D characters could expect to tackle!

Gamma World's character types are the tip-off that this is an intrinsically different game from D&D. D&D core character classes try to cover all the bases. The fightingman class, inspired by Edgar Rice Burroughs's *John Carter of Mars* and Robert E. Howard's *Conan*, typically serves as point man during dungeon delves. The fighter leads the way in all things related to bashing heads. The magic-user class derived from Jack Vance's weird far future *Dying Earth* tales is a sort of limited-ammunition artillery piece that must be positioned carefully and protected by other player characters in order to be effective. The thief class's amalgam of abilities drawn from Vance's *Cugel the Clever*, Leiber's *The Grey Mouser*, and Zelazny's *Jack of Shadows* make him the ideal scout who provides the party with critical intelligence needed to avoid arbitrary death and fruitless combat. The cleric, finally, drawing inspiration from an unprecedented combination of Van Helsing and the Knights Templar, somehow manages to free all the other classes up to do what they do best.

The way the core character classes of classic D&D complement each other is arguably one of the greatest developments of gaming history. They have an air of inevitability about them—perhaps even a Platonic purity. It's difficult to imagine how fantasy role-playing could even work without them—so naturally *Gamma World* dispenses with them entirely. In their place is some truly weird stuff.

First there is the Pure Strain Human who has none of the signature mutant abilities for which the game is known for. In theory, he should be the equal of the other character types thanks to his comprehension of ancient artifacts, his increased charisma, byproduct of the awe his physical purity produces. Furthermore, will not be bothered by robots guarding the best technological loot. Players who opt for this type will be sidelined unless the referee specifically sets up the game world to accommodate them.

Next come the mutants, Humanoids and Mutant Animals. They get one to four physical and mental mutations each. The abilities are assigned according to these hilariously baroque d100 tables that never fail to produce something that's both amusing and fun to play. Whatever faults this game might have, they are more than made up for by the greatness of its random mutant abilities. The main difference between Humanoids and Animals is the animals cannot use tools or weapons beyond their mutant abilities. To make up for this, they receive some "natural" attack forms and abilities which are nowhere delineated in the rules.

The final character type is something of an afterthought: the Mutated Plants. They were not an option for player characters in the first edition of the game and, in the third edition, they appear to have only just barely made it into the game at all. Mutants of this type get fewer mutations than either Humanoids or Mutant Animals making them the obvious red-headed stepchild of the character type lineup.

Turn this game over to a typical group of adolescents in the late 1980s and hilarity necessarily ensues. Some mutations are straightforward abilities drawn from the animal kingdom—quills, antlers, sound imitation, chameleon powers, and so on. Others are psionic abilities drawn from science fiction stories: mental blasts, telekinesis, teleportation, and pyrokinesis. Still others could have been taken verbatim from the pages of classic X-men comics: density control, wings, total healing, skeletal enhancement, magnetic control, and weather manipulation. Then there are the truly weird abilities like planar opening and time manipulation which don't fit into any of those categories!

Anything goes with this game. If the character abilities aren't weird enough, they get even stranger when put together in random combinations. Roll up a mutant bear with military genius, telekinetic flight, and gas generation? That would be Napoleon Bonafart, naturally. *Gamma World* characters immediately take on a life of their own.

While *Gamma World* has a freaky internal logic that emerges over the course of play, it would have been nevertheless difficult to imagine the literary and cinematic basis from which arise the spirit of the rules. The game was just too weird! About the only thing on the shelves at the local Walden Books back then that would have come close would have maybe been a couple of Alan Dean Foster novels that would have been in the ballpark of the game's premise—

Midworld or *Escape from Prism*, for example. It might as well have been a completely original genre unto itself for all the typical eighties kid would have known.

Gamers lucky enough to come across a copy of the first edition of the game published in the dark era that was 1978 would be privy to the strange impetus of the game. It's broken down explicitly in the forward:

> Drawing inspiration from such works as *The Long Afternoon of Earth* by Brian Aldiss, *Starman's* [sic] *Son* by Andre Norton, *Hiero's Journey* by Sterling Lanier, and Ralph Bakshi's animated feature film "Wizards," the referee of a *Gamma World* campaign fleshes out the game, adding any details he or she deems necessary, and thereby creating a unique world in which day-to-day survival is in doubt. These rules are flexible enough to allow for a variety of approaches to the game—anything from a strictly "hard" science-fiction attention to physical probabilities to a free-flowing Bakshian combination of science-fiction and fantasy. It is relatively simple to integrate these rules with *Advanced Dungeons & Dragons* and/or *Metamorphosis: Alpha To Omega* as they were edited with this in mind.

The treasure trove of works listed there are astonishingly heterogeneous. And as far as inspirations for a second- tier game title goes, this one can't be beat.

Norton's *Star Man's Son* is the most conventional. A humanoid and his mutant animal companion strike off into the Blow-up Lands to loot ruins irradiated by a relatively recent nuclear war. Once a pure strain human joins their adventures, all three original character types of the game are accounted for, along with a mainstay of *Gamma World* campaigns: the tenuous survival of a variety of hardscrabble tribes and creatures on the cusp of returning to the stars. Lanier's *Hiero's Journey* is the most broadly influential in the world of early role-playing games. The iconic green slime of original D&D hails from these pages. The rabbit-derived mounts called Hoops were appropriated from this book for *Gamma World*, as was a key aspect of the alien Droyne culture of classic Traveller. The pure strain humans of this novel depart from *Gamma World* rules by having psychic powers rather than access to advanced technologies from before the apocalypse. On the other hand, the mutant animal characters here embody everything *Gamma World* takes for granted about them. The apocalypse is dated much further back than in *Star Man's Son*. There are fewer cities to loot than is typically taken for granted in *Gamma World* campaigns. However, Lanier's world has had enough time to steep so that something akin to *Gamma World*'s freaky, secret and semi-secret societies, called "cryptic alliances", have had a chance to develop.

Ralph Bakshi's "Wizards" is the ultimate example of how fantasy and science fiction were viewed quite dif ferently not that long ago. Granted, the pitched battle between a sorcerous dark lord and his wizardly nemesis are reminiscent of the Tolkienesque works that would become ubiquitous in the early eighties. But *Elf Quest*-style short elves teaming up with faerie and cyborg bounty hunters in a science vs. magic free-for-all where the game-changing epic McGuffin is a collection of Nazi war propaganda able to galvanize the morale of a coalition of orcs and gas mask wearing, laser rifle toting humans? That's a whole new level of weirdness right there! (Bonus: anyone that has ever been puzzled by the inclusion of *Gamma World* conversion rules with the first edition AD&D *Dungeon Master's Guide* can now see for themselves why this was de rigueur at the time.)

And then there is the Brian Aldiss title, *The Long Afternoon of Earth*, more commonly known as *Hothouse*. Unlike the other *Gamma World* inspirations, this one presents an over-the-top mutant future that isn't triggered by a nuclear exchange in the wake of an out-ofcontrol population explosion. The moral failings of humanity are both insignificant and irrelevant here. Aldiss dispenses with the usual patronizing cautionary tale altogether and instead extrapolates a world where time and evolutionary forces are sufficient to create an awesomely weird earth teeming with fantastic plant-life.

The sun of the *Hothouse* Earth puts out orders of magnitude more radiation as it slouches towards supernova. The planet has stopped turning on its axis and the continent on the sun-facing side is dominated by a single gargantuan tree. Mankind is reduced to savagery, living in tiny tribes huddled in the treetops, beset by a menagerie of carnivorous plants and the occasional giant insect. Above the forest canopy, spider-like mega-flora spin webs that reach up into space. Driven by instinct, humans that are long in the tooth encase themselves into seed pods while their tribe attaches them to the legs of these "spiders." From there, they "go up" whereupon these elders are deposited on the moon where they undergo a metamorphosis, turning into winged flymen that return to earth to steal the children of the isolated tribes of man!

This fix-up of science fiction magazine novellas delivers everything that the more degenerate elements of fandom clamored for in the 1940s. No white Anglo- Saxon protestants appear anywhere in the pages of this book. Indeed, the main protagonists are all greenskinned and stunted. There are no feats of derring-do or heroism. The males of humanity are in short supply and thus undergo a stark role-reversal from what we expect today. Women take on leadership roles and lead in battle as well, while men are treated like a priceless reproductive resource. Those yearning for a realistic take on alternative sexualities the future could potentially hold get a glimpse of a completely normalized polygamy, with most taboos of twentieth century America either inverted or dispensed with entirely.

Of course, this gamma-male wish-fulfillment fantasy can hardly be said to be an advancement over 1950s middle America. Aldiss's hyper-progressive take on far-future marriage arrangements are predicated on mankind being so collectively brain damaged by intense solar radiation that they lose all vestiges of culture, civilization, and technology. Fortunately, the darker side of science fiction fandom only rarely intrudes on the storytelling.

There are creatures here unlike any that I have ever seen in any *Gamma World* campaign. Trees that extract sulfur, charcoal, and potassium nitrite from the ground in order to make gunpowder-infused seed pods. "Burnurns" that grow lenses that can harness sunlight into deadly energy blasts. "Tummy-trees" that grow cords that attach to the bellies of humanoids, allowing them to exchange their freedom for easy sustenance. Oak trees that drop wooden cages on their prey from above, fertilizing the ground with the remains of their captives. Octopus- like "killerwillows" that can tunnel through sand. "Bellyelms" that appear to be decaying, hollowed out logs but which digest any creature that takes refuge within it.

Aldiss's creativity is positively boundless. He comes up with no less than six distinct ecological environments— the hothouse proper, the moon, the border zone between hothouse and sea, two distinctive islands, and finally, the Big Slope, a twilight region beyond a span of darkness. One recurring plot device here is the use of plants for rapid transportation: odd spinner-seeds that come when called, bird-like plant creatures, and six-legged walking seed pods. In a world lacking traditional science fiction technologies, plants are shown to be more than able to fill the void.

However, there is one "ancient" artifact which the human protagonists stumble across. The passage describing their completely random interactions with it was no doubt an inspiration for *Gamma World*'s Artifact Examination Chart:

> Fashioned of strange materials, of metals and plastics, the insides of the yellow bird were marvelous to behold. Here were small spools, a line of knobs, a glimpse of amplifying circuits, a maze of running intestines. Full of curiosity, the two humans leant forward to touch. Full of wonder, they let their fingers—those four fingers with opposed thumb that had taken their ancestors so far— enjoy the delight of toggle switches. The tuning knobs could be twiddled, the switches clicked!

Solving the puzzle of how to activate it turns out to be very amusing thanks to Aldiss's dry British wit. And the flying Heckler drone turns out to be completely useless in regard to helping deliver characters out of trouble. It merely hovers in their vicinity periodically shouting things like "Stand up for your rights while you still have them", "Don't get caught between Delhi bureaucracy and Communist intrigues", "Boycott chimp goods", and "Think for yourselves and vote SRH!"

In *Hothouse* there is no remnant of humanity that will be able to return to former glory, no ancient artifact foretold by prophecy, and no weapons cache replete with everything necessary to rescue princesses or carve out a modest empire from these future jungles. Everything that ever mattered to that decadent civilization that once ruled the earth is shown to be puerile, fleeting, and vain. Aldiss delivers nothing that his predecessors writing tales of pulpy adventure would have taken for granted, but he at least turned out to be the sort of writer who believed he should offer something equally compelling in its place. In this case, that something evidently left enough of an impression on Gamma World's designers that they felt compelled to accommodate it.

Third edition Gamma World actually includes a special variant of the mutated plant called the symbiot which "must inhabit an unintelligent mobile creature to gain many of the benefits of free action." It was not a particularly inviting option for play, honestly. The designers take special pains to artificially limit them, requiring that they "inhabit only common animals when it first begins the game" and forbidding them from changing hosts until their original host dies. The rules supplement goes further, piling on additional penalties on the symbiot's rolls for hit point and drastically limiting the allowable hit dice amounts of its host.

This is a far cry from the creature Aldiss actually envisioned. His morel mushroom symbiot was the impetus for mankind's development of larger skulls, and the key that unlocked their intelligence. The extinction of man's "other half" from increases in solar radiation was so catastrophic, it ended civilization and reduced man to a plant-like lifestyle and a low animal intelligence. The morel would eventually kill its hosts. But it could also change hosts at will if it could get into position to drop onto them. If it had grown large enough, it could potentially divide, thereby taking over multiple creatures simultaneously. Finally, taking over a creature gave it access to not only the creature's personal knowledge and life experiences, but its ancestral memories as well.

There was no limit on the size of the creatures the symbiot could take over—even those gigantic spider creatures weaving webs that reached up to the moon were fair game. And therein lies the greatest twist of the novel: a morel mushroom that did so became the solution to *Gamma World*'s built-in campaign objective. It became a plant technology replacement for spacecraft. With a symbiot controlling a space-faring creature, it could navigate the vacuum of space, providing man with an incredible escape from a doomed Earth.

Properly played, a character with such abilities should be able to break almost any conceivable Gamma World campaign. On the other hand, today's obsession with play balance is notably absent in a game that routinely produces over-the-top, crazily overpowered characters. Something closer to Brian Aldiss's symbiot would have fit right in and been a lot of fun to boot.

Fortunately, prospective referees up to the task can easily rectify this minor error in tabletop's finest science fantasy role-playing game. For a game that is predicated on cranking the weirdness up to eleven, running it any other way would be doing it wrong.

ROOT HOG OR DIE

Neal Durando

My smart head is me talking. I talk mostly like Gordo taught me but also from books. Fact of the matter is I talk—mostly—only to Gordo. My palette is wide so I kind of huff it out. Gordo calls my other head the stupid head. Because it speaks worse. I've got less teeth. So I call it the stupid head, too. Its real name is Walbur. My stupid head takes in the sun, casts about for the bright Shepherd's Star, or ponders the green moon while I think about the speed of light and how to stop time, make it go back. (Oh, would that it could all go back.) Walbur is just along for the ride, as I usually get the legs. He gazes on sow haunches steeped in filth and reels down our pizzle while my smart head, me, tries to figure out the best way to follow Gordo into the bottoms and the easiest drag route back to Yam Farm. When I hear my smart name, I turn my smart head. "Wilbar," says Gordo one morning, "Want to go after the green sounder again?"

The kids have been wandering up from Yam Town with hungry looks. Bruto with the extra baby arm and Fales, his face awash in a red rash presaging dry weather. So long as it isn't Skaggs bearing his guns. More of them cry at the door every evening. We slop them over to their side of the fence to keep them from getting ideas about climbing. The way up from Yam Town is usually far enough to make them indifferent. A body loses more calories than you get from us if you walk over our way. Our yams are in but aren't ready for me to unroot them. We've waited since planting for those wild pigs, the green sounder, to come back to the part of the bottoms near Yam Farm. Five or six generations of them wander the wilds. Something went wrong with the world a long time ago so that they're green. Maybe it was the same for the moon. They're all the same shade. So is everyone under moonshine but most of us go back to black and white by day. A lot of things could be explained by whatever went wrong. That the lizards in all the books are such small things, bearing no resemblance to those of today. The kids today with two rows of teeth. The very existence of jagwares maybe owes to some older sin. Gordo just grabs the spear he uses on boars and he's out of the hole.

Gordo knows no fear and I know none, either. So long as I am with Gordo I can strike out. There isn't even time to look for Twitchy Henry and tell him to bring his stretch band. Walbur, his mouth full of yam heart, picked up on my excitement. I felt his ear flick against mine. Gordo is already across the creek where the bottoms begin by the time we get the legs in gear. I hope he remembers to put out the board so I won't have to swim, as I'm no good on moss rocks.

Behold Gordo by dawn's early light with the goggles on his face. They erase his eyes though you would be a fool to imagine him blind; the black pools made by the lenses make you fear that his sockets might just turn out to be empty. Gordo standing in the glimmer with his boar spear is a force of precision, like lightning, when it comes to opening a pig body. As many times as I've seen him kill, I can recognize the tension that overtakes him on the day he gets the idea to hunt. He looks like he just jumped out of the bush. Maybe his inner driver is simple hunger, like anyone else. But suppose it is something else. I admit that looking upon Gordo as a hunter in his home mode makes the spot where my neck joins with Walbur a bit itchy.

I could slip out, watch the constellations wane then disappear while Walbur inhales yam husks. I could just let him do the legs thereafter, but then I wouldn't be following

Gordo. And what would be the sense in that? Besides the sows, in spite of their toxic color, I just want to eat their long teats right up. On this alone, Walbur and I may be said to be of one mind.

"We'll see farther from the top of Weed Hill," I huff out at Gordo's back. He is already halfway up. Sometimes I wonder if he hears me at all. Or stops to listen. Sometimes I wonder if I can read his thoughts, if only for a few minutes after he has them. Like the morning stars, Gordo's intentions wane away. It's a little like how Twitchy Henry is always where you least expect him. And, after you spot him, how it seems as if he were there all along. Lots of crazy stuff goes on around Yam Town if you keep your every sense awake. One thing. Maybe I, my smart head, is to Gordo as my stupid head is to myself. Whatever. I know I'm hard to follow. If not going after Gordo for all he's worth, I find myself going in circles.

When Gordo gets in his hunting way, a kind of all–over tension invades him. He spits in the goggles, cleans them, works a dial on the side until they whine. You begin to see muscles come out of his back. Sometimes he gets so tight he can't see his way around the whole hunt. He'll walk too far on a dogleg path, barely get back before dark, having given up on a cold laughter flower or brutorz. Or he takes a path through the bottoms so overgrown we can't tow the meat bag through. I hate the times he throws his spear. It always means hours of dipping my nose into strange blood. The trail always leads somewhere scratchy. Usually, the sun sits on the broken horizon and we can smell the howlers, maybe even a lizard. By the time Gordo drags the hook chain out of the meat bag and we are down to regular slogging. But Walbur smiles in the face of any weather and under the drag of any yoke no matter the weight.

I guess I draw some strength off Walbur which offsets the dull, constant burden of his brotherhood. Twitchy Henry is more worrisome. He'll take a shot from atop a cliff or oak with the stretch band. He yells while the bullet is still humming in the air. They stop and wonder at the sound. Henry's yawp riding above a nearing buzz is their last music before they are stricken to the dust, jowls tight with acorns. Henry will yell right along with a squealing juvenile as it falls. I guess he doesn't have to love one or the other. Henry harmonizes to both killing and death. I'll watch from under a dwarf oak and encourage him when it's time to come down and butcher. Henry bitches a lot about his knees. Steep grades aren't my cup of tea, either.

Mornings, there are never any howlers on the wind.

Gordo is already through the lower wallow. He has left out the plank. We plonk across and begin postholing in his steps. I don't dare take the time to cool my balls in the mud like I usually do here after dragging out the sacks of corn and husks that the kids spread about. Gordo's moccasin holes are already leading through pools of luminescent urine left by the green sounder. From my side eye, I see Fales following. He gnaws a dry cob with his ruined teeth, sees me, goes away angry. Once, Gordo staked out a goat here. He wanted to attract a lizard, wanted to go Gordo-a-Monstro. Or so he said. It never showed. Finally, Twitchy Henry blasted the horns off the poor goat out of sheer boredom. And because they were rotten with weed.

The killing ground is set up so Gordo has a clear track to run straight down. He stays just behind the speed of his legs and yells like a howler or some even more basic force. Like lightning. Or Laughing Plague. Whatever. He sounds like something that could steal life just as fast. Wild ones—lizards, the kids with no names, presumably jagwares—just go around in the moment. Catching sight of anything is like a first time. They never learn. We always set up in the same place.

For now, he sits on my back and we are listening, me with my nose. The weed is high. As is the hill. Gathered together, we are all lordly over the bottom land. This is no time but now. My nose hears the green sounder is pissing a short trot upwind. Twitchy Henry emerges from the buds and branches at a regal moment once we have grown comfortable. He installs himself on the scene as if he's been here all along. I wouldn't wonder if he had a shack back there somewhere. It is as if he has always lived on Weed Hill. You can never tell with Henry. So long as you don't hear him bitching about his rotator cuff first, he might show up pretty much out of anywhere.

I can smell the sounder under the spruce. Gordo gets up. I can make out exactly where they will emerge into a brake. By the tank whose seepage waters the lower wallow. My spine serves as Gordo's compass. I turn myself toward the place and hope he follow the point of the smart head. In spite of their weird color, they are delicious to contemplate by twilight. There's a young sow, especially, still lithe after her first litters. She is as green as the moon at lunar springtime, save for the chic white belt across her withers. All animals bear visible signs of error, nowadays. Each in their particular error cannot compare with their color–plate ancestors in the book. The jagware can presumably change colors, Twitchy Henry says. Or else members of animalia range wider than where you'd expect to find them. Snow bears, mangy and exhausted, are not unknown in our arid environs. It is no surprise that a creature eat the flesh of men, where before it was fruit and seed. So at least we're spared that. New animals appear. Some have crossed over from plants. You couldn't possibly keep up. She, green as she may be, would stand out in anyone's book, day or night. Although we are upwind, it will be a while before they wander over to spear range.

"Make me a pipe, Twitchy Henry?" I ask. He usually carries an extra stem in the front pocket of his overalls. Henry strips me off a fist of weed straight from the stalk, balls it up, packs it down with his hard thumb.

"That's right decent, Twitchy Henry." I have to thank him quickly because the brothers can forget half way through doing me a kindness. The worst thing I can think of is being forgotten in the hole overnight, unfed.

"Creation sure creates some weird creatures," says Gordo, half asleep. He's watching the sounder ease out into the brake one by one. They're filing down into the wallow, confident yet shambolic. The white corn we scattered stands out on the mud very well in the gloom. You've got to get over how Gordo uses the same word in a sentence. "If it ain't broke it ain't broke, ain't broke, ain't it?" makes sense once you let it roll around in your head long enough. I don't mind because his quirks give me a chance to put a pin in whatever he's talking about so I can look it up later. You take what you can get, remember what you can, if you rely on others to turn the pages of your storybooks.

Henry maneuvers the pipe past my tusks, puts it in my jaw, lights it up. Walbur groans and falls into a clouded dream. Henry gets it right every time. Mostly, my stupid head is for stupid stuff like weed, but I like a pipe myself, now and then. Henry gives my stupid head a scratch, which makes it grunt. I waggle the stem on the bar of my jaw. I try to get it to jut out like Gordo when he's picking stones in the field. That way I can still talk.

The sounder shies off in little groups, gathers again, then moves closer to our position en masse. I cannot imagine what draws them away on their little errands. Myself, watching in weed stupor, I would go from kernel to kernel to kernel, following the diktats of the most efficient line. But a sounder is always unsettled. Your average pig takes a year to grow out of the shadow of its mother. You can never tell why a boar cuts for the trees or how many will follow. I try to send my mind down to them but I only get back hunger. You might think the older ones, the ones that keep themselves distant, are wiser. But that's not how life in the bottoms works. True bottom life be beyond such beasts. Those boars are just survivors with no guarantee beyond the day. They go from kernel to kernel. A geometrical function to predict their movement begins to bother my head. There is a best path through. I can spot points of indifference, a least-distance matrix, but then it gets too baroque. This weed is far too sweet.

And then, like moonshine from behind parting clouds, there they are, undivided, monocephalic, uncloven, luminescent, green. You can make up words sometimes if you know how the parts of them meet. The males board the sows between mouthfuls. The girls, even while mounted, never stop eating. There's no logic to it that I can tell. Eat then screw. Eat while screwing. I wish I could make my own pipe. All I would need are thumbs. The sweet pipe draws cold. "All done," says my stupid head, for all the world like a dutiful child. I open my yap and let the cob fall from my jaw. "Wait a sec," I say. A clever shoat with good ears raises its head, squeals a warning too sharp for anyone to mind, and scampers away, drawing his smarter sisters and brothers in his wake. These will be tonight's survivors. New sounders are created from moments of liquid fear like this. The spectacle—and Gordo on my back—give me a headache. The weed could use less fertilizer. Far too sweet. Put out less corn. Damn it. I can't whisper.

Oh, for thumbs.

Oh, for a sow.

Getting up the lungs to huff a whisper makes a notion of gas pass out of me with a loud pop.

Gordo always gets in first. He stood, straight away off my back, and was gone before I could say "Run girls! Here comes Gordo!" I had those very words formed up and ready to go in my smart head. Gouts of snot jet from my stupid snout as it wakes. The banded sow had turned scattering her shoats at her feet. I swear I can hear her thinking "Who is this handsome devil?" Meaning me. She fixes on Gordo already on his way down, takes the measure of him, charges. But she cannot make good speed up the grade. He meets her half way down his special run. His spear goes straight into the sassy white band I so admired. The point finds her heart because of course it does. She slides straight back to the bottom, legs stiff in sharp surprise. She can no longer do harm to Gordo. Gordo, for his part, cannot avoid following through, vaulting through the air, ass over tea kettle, her body now a fulcrum. He slams down into the mud upon his back, startling the shoats out farther. I'm sure I catch the white crescent of his grin while in the air. Nobody misses his victory yawp.

Honestly, you would think that I know how to speak to pigs. You could dust off your best word, put it together with your second best, stay off the weed, and take the time to articulate, but you'd get nothing back. Animals wiggle around by noises and smells. Words can mean too many things. Or are just noise. She was just dead, the spear ticking in time with her heart as her every motive ebbed away. I wonder if I might speak better if I hadn't wording. Who forces this compromise? Woe is the animal world.

Twitchy Henry *thoks* his stretch band at the rest of them until the corn is glowed over with the sounder's green essence. An old shouldery porker dies, kissed on the forehead by a bullet's smack. His sagely jowls are no protection. Then the unchosen run on a ways, forget why they are running, halt, return to rooting out corn, to their illusions, the table we set for them. Gordo makes me another bowl to smoke in the time it takes for Twitchy Henry to tire.

"You look sad," Gordo says to my smart side.

"Sorry," I say, "I'm blasted."

Gordo pats my stupid head, gets a grunt out of it. "Be easy. Tonight we eat well. Maybe beyond."

I guess what brings them back is the smell of corn and yams. It overcomes the smoke and blood, so loud is the hunger inside them. Hell, I almost go down myself. Glowing green mud festoons from between their trotters. They nudge their own brothers' stiff, air-leg corpses, set down to feeding again. Someone should say words. But what would those words be? No warning would stick. Twitchy Henry takes his time and makes his choice, thoks another bullet out beyond my thickening focus. There is a scramble, a squeal, a hush. It sure is getting late. The dead shine out their light, limning out the limit of Henry's stones toward the bush, the little green hills of them as far as I can make out.

"Why you got to kill so many?" I ask Henry while he's winding down. "What was the insult? How hungry are the kids? Who hurt you?" Gordo is away up the hill, making extra balls of weed for me to carry back in the meat bag. Twitchy Henry is attaching the drag chains to our harness. I was already at labor, chewing on new questions.

"I just want them to stand still," says Twitchy

Henry. I thought he had ignored my question. His eyes are shy from me. His voice was soft and close to my ear. He was talking to someone else past me, though. Or someone even closer. "I want them still so I can get a better look," said Henry. By then, the smoke was beginning to wear off. I was growing cross. He spooned the carcasses together, hocks to rump, sized down from sows to boars to shoats. "They're different when they're all together," he said, "You can run your fingers on their scars. Puzzle out the history of their fights. You can open their jaws and get a load of their teeth."

"There's no place any better?" I ask, "Out there?"

"It ain't pattern without error," says Twitchy Henry, with his thumbs hooked in my sow's mouth. I don't know whether he means the jagged line of her teeth or the line of ridges above the bottoms. Then I don't see him any longer, although I am looking right at him. I know we'll catch up with each other at Yam Farm, because that's the way we usually do. You can be looking at Henry one moment and in the next you're just remembering him. He just fades out of your eyes. The absence makes Walbur grunt. I suppose it is okay to fuss a bit when you are confused.

Gordo pats at the water in the tank. The slick off his hands glows and fades as it spreads across the surface. "Time to head back to the hole, Wilbar," he says.

He's got them all hooked up now. The ones he wanted. That night, I dragged for everyone,

Yam Farm, Yam Town. I pondered some on death on the way. How they all danced a little different. Gordo piled them on rails made of sticks lashed. Death got into them in different ways. He tied the sticks to my withers and then the chains. They keeled if struck clean. Or wheeled in the air if running. Often, the green pigs stopped suddenly as if you had tapped them on the shoulder. If struck at deflection or with English no animal is so very spectacular. They all have their own way of going out of nature. Some hop up higher than they ever could in life. Some roll, especially birds. Some just stop in the air, while others skid to a stop on their chins. This is the case of pigs, but I've also seen a howler plant his face. The kill is a trick you play on them from the bushes atop Weed Hill, a moment where it is better them than you. Tree rats scamper in every direction almost forever as they have to nose at every object one last time. You would think a cave bear would turn toward you, claw revenge out of your fleeing. I know I did. But in truth they go off wounded toward their grotto, guilty and ashamed. I saw one, in full flight, shit out a red flag of the blood berries it had been eating. Turkerlies just get pinned to the ground and pivot to a stop. A goat just keeps walking on its way, grumpy as ever, until it drops. Deer go big through the brush, raise sideways dust, crash down small trees. Death is a big deal for the deer but less so for goats. Jump cats bleed out while stranded upon high branches, which is the only place you can kill them. Gordo has to climb up to get them. Or else you go on, let them go to bones, retrieve the useful skull come autumn. We went back in our trace. It ain't pattern without error. I think it's a dance. I wondered what Walbur made of it, but he made no outward sign. We have never ever seen a jagware. The brutorz looks up a little, as if puzzled by a bee sting but does not otherwise move until the end. You'd be forgiven for thinking blood would stir everyone more than it does. When I look back, what I see is he had put a hook under the sow's jawbone at the end. She's heaviest but rigging it this way ensures the chain draws straight. So we were together, with the green moon above, Gordo and I. I have long moments to find my words. We're stopped at the upper wallow, drinking from the cool branch.

"Why," I ask, "Is Twitchy Henry such an intemperate murderer?" I figured Gordo would just shrug and say "Nature of the beast," as he does when encountering something disagreeable which he has no power to change. He doesn't answer right away. We go on a ways in the glow. It was pretty much a straight drag from here. Walbur was half asleep and so I put all four ears on Gordo.

"We got down into the bottoms once," says Gordo. "We go out for days, slogged beyond the yams we could carry. Had to live on snare meat. Grubbers and jumpers. We lost our boots. We were walking on skins. There's a gum tree out there, white in the middle against everything else. Full of rats or something like them, all tail and action. They were going up and down the gum tree, not noticing us very much. Henry gets out his stretch band."

"As he does," I said. Sometimes Gordo needs to be invited to continue.

"As he does," agrees Gordo, "Henry's long out of bullets, so he fetches up a stone, clicks his tongue to make one of the small creatures stop and look. Knocks the thing's head clean off. Just chunks it, sidearm." Gordo postholes back, unsnags the sow and flips her over a deadfall, returns, and takes up where he left off. "Rats are all stirred up now, running in pairs on equal opposite sides of the gum tree trunk. We could see them clear on the white bark but we couldn't justly see what they were after. Henry went on down just to retrieve that little scrap of meat. They were in quite a whirl. The rats were going down to visit their brother with their noses for half a second. They wouldn't quit the gum tree even with Henry looming over. Something about their chatter or maybe their toes on the bark." Gordo drew up, concentrating for a moment. "'The scatter got into my eyes.' That's how he put it. He had to slide down with his back to the trunk and sleep. And he got to flailing, Wilbar, like you've never seen him do. I went down myself and took care of him past dark. All those rats complained at me from under the crown. I skinned and ate their brother with no fire.

Henry was gone in the morning. It was the first time he ever pulled that. I thought he'd been taken off. On the way home, I got used to him being gone forever."

"I'll warrant he is special touched," I say, lamely. We go down the lane between the yam fields. I don't know what else to say. I'm too tired to sound smart. We're almost to the hole.

"He can't lose track," says Gordo, "A fear comes over him when faced with too much movement. Nature of the beast."

Light spills from the shed. Gordo draws the blanket across, extinguishing it save for the little stars and lines that appear at its limit. Walbur is snoring and our balls are back in the mud. I smell pig's blood more clearly than I can see the moon going down over Yam Town. I can hear Skaggs roaring, drunk on horse apple wine. Gordo doesn't bring the lamp once he's done. I'm too gone for reading, anyway. I can hear the bucket.

"Chow's on," says Gordo. He yawns, standing above me holding a pail. "Parts," he says.

A cascade of trotters and snouts, all the stuff he can't be bothered to further disjoin or render, falls across the moon into our little wallow. I can see where they all land. Walbur stirs. I am so damn hungry.

"Go," says Gordo, "Get at it."

Walbur wakes full, of a sudden like a siren, fills the early morning air with a baby's scream.

❖

We're way out past the last mud. It is all I can do to keep dust enough on me. Walbur keeps swallowing his tongue and then spitting it out. I would like to do our whole back in better dust. We are so dry now nothing sticks. I can't do anything to stop Walbur with his tongue. We'd both be better off keeping our yaps shut in this heat. Walbur sounds like the Yam Farm donkey engine getting up steam. I doubt he has any idea we're in the desert, that there could be a place containing nothing. Maybe he lets his jawbone hang open of sheer disbelief. Now and then he clacks his lower tusks against the uppers. Nothing he does helps matters. "Walbur!" I snap. He shuts it until he catches sight of a spider in the shadow of an overhang. We haven't had a drink all day. The dust keeps falling off.

Twitchy Henry says we're already a day too deep in the wrong direction. The far-hearinged kid, Fales, just looks at me when I asked about water, did he hear any raindrops or subterranean flow. "You do you," said Fales. When they don't care whether you live or die this is what the kids say. Gordo gives no sign to turn back, so I'm not turning back, either. So long as I've got the legs. Walbur and I are going to be tasting the black smear of a spider he just swallowed for a long while. At least my mouth is clean.

I sleep only in short stretches. Every wakeup it is either Walbur or me. We wouldn't survive a day in the desert walking circles as we do

when I sleep late at Yam Farm. Here, the sun is high and Gordo moves on early. I'm worried about our back. We should go do a roll, but it is easier just to keep walking. I think some of the kids have peeled off. Maybe even gone to glory. They do them, before all. Gordo keeps on straight toward the Shepherd's Star without letting on or up. We didn't leave Yam Farm early enough all those days ago. That's why so many kids tag along. We all follow Gordo and Gordo follows his star so long as I don't have to fight for the legs. I don't want to find out where we'd end up if Walbur got the jump on me in the morning. If he can smell water he isn't letting on. Maybe he is out beyond caring as far as I am.

One morning, we are present for a new star's rise. It is just Gordo and me and Walbur, still lolling his head half in a dream. We're already walking. At first, I think it is the same old Shepherd's Star, bright as distant water. It rises from the flat horizon, and then goes off track, quick like Skaggs's unreliable Holiday rockets, changing to a bright green as it goes. Gordo stops and traces its progress with his whole arm. Gordo's arm is straight up and it turns white. Gordo blows it out as if the rising star were a ball of dander weed. Or a spark of his own striking.

"Signs and wonders," says Twitchy Henry from somewhere behind us out in the dark.

"Knew I was on to something, Henry," says Gordo, as if they were alone.

I flip my ears around and can hear some of Fales's kids crabbing up. Gosh, they are no fun. Even Walbur looks the other way. "My dudes!" chirps Fales, "Was that lit or what?" Meaning, I suppose, the rising star. "Whadeye miss?" implores a hulking fatty in the timbre of a daunted child. "Sucks to be you," says his mate, a twerp wearing a monocle. Nobody knows how many of the kids there are. And we can never get up early enough to leave them behind. To what are they drawn? What drives them? Go figure. We try not to speak to them.

We come up on rocks. Twitchy Henry stops. I feel we're at our limit. I would stay beside him if I thought he was turning around for Yam Town. Or if Henry was ever interested in water. Once, I tried to keep him company. All he does is touch every rock. He goes through this like a duty before he can take up the track again. Or even look up. He doesn't talk, except to murmur while running his palms over every stone and passing his fingers through the sand. His conjury occupies the whole of him. Maybe he's only counting. Maybe there's a chapter and verse to it. Or the rules of stones. I got worried once I started losing Gordo's scent and left him. Eventually, Henry always works his way back, usually after sundown, his gourd full, his belly round, his stride easy. Sometimes he wets our back if I'm not already rutted in and dead to the world. One morning he left me a wet yam.

At night, I can smell the kids camp, a wide,

fetid ring around us. Who knows how far out in the dark they are? When I rut ourselves in, following the inescapable instinct for circles, there is no point on the horizon not smeared by their reek. Their filth overwhelms any breeze such that the wind becomes strange to itself and seems to issue from oblique directions. Wilbar even closes his fool mouth when it blows hard. They shit everywhere. Their voices carry, raised. A pair of cretins, Turgon and Erenzo, were swatting sparks into each other's' hair with smoldering brands. "Fire is elite only," explained Turgon to Erenzo. I suppose there was some kind of prize for getting up flames first. "Elite only is fire," responds Erenzo. Out there, they shriek like donkeys, play grab-ass, get up imprudently massive bonfires, sear and eat everything they can find. All the sapwood bears evidence of their teeth. Also, it's sub-lizards, the knee-high ones, going by the stink. Beneath it all, like a snake in the crib, roils the smell of howlers.

After fighting for their meals, after eating, they split up or go out chattering in their new subtribes for various night reasons. These kids, they are not alright. They laugh at anything and everything, reel with each other's girls, pull their beards into forks, strike the fire higher. Our lot is to lie still, endure. They squeak like mice when they screw, even the ones with ruined chests and impeccable mustaches. How do they stay plump when yours truly has grown so narrow?

"Stick it in," we hear through laughter. "Break it off," comes the response. The spurned come from the outer dark to stir those about the fire or else scare them straight into the flames. When a towering bonfire collapses, victims run about in the flames. The kids are always burning and laughing and dying, more so than other animals I've seen. Fang deer in heat comport themselves with more dignity. Lizards fuck less and, at any rate, do not write rude slogans on each other's bodies.

A girl named Joyz seeks to slip a lacy bonnet onto Walbur while he dozes. I lie awake, watching, wondering if she will continue her approach upon seeing the light in my eye. I have time to think about what to say.

"Knock your taco in the dirt," I growl. This is the meanest thing I can think of. (Imagine!) Joyz's nose was held together with studs, as one does with swine or slaves. A surprised expression flicked across her face, crusty with infection.

"You mad little bruh?" says Joyz. She goes ahead and gets the bonnet over Walbur's ears. I don't know why this was supposed to be funny, but out there someone is hooting. I felt the electricity of my brother's waking. I let go of the legs, let him charge. Got ourselves a piece of Joyz's leg I can still taste. Her pain raises more laughter. I have the feeling there are a lot more wagers among them still.

We never got the bonnet off.

All these antics draw challenges from the

howlers, a pack of which have been following us since we walked out of Yam Trace Draw. I imagine them gathering to us in bird view, an ever-wider ring of dark forms beyond the kids' shambolic camp. Mostly, the kids remain by the wrecked fire, heedless of howler calls. Those things out there know the sun takes more from us than the night can put back. Everything rays out form where Gordo decides to bed down.

The one who calls herself Winona, had a baby the night before we saw the second star. ("Wormwood," Twitchy Henry called it.) Winona yelled long and loud and louder until she was joined by her child's keening in the moon shadow. Winona whelped under an outcrop looking down upon flat hardpan across which, by day, lay an assortment of gigantic bones. I could smell howlers nearing on her grotto. I suppose they were desperate to lap at the water Winona had let out. Honestly, I wouldn't have minded doing so myself, such was my thirst. I turned Walbur to the escarpment wall before my distasteful idea could zap over to him. Out of sight, out of mind.

"What on earth are mother and child going to do?" I ask Twitchy Henry, perched above us, with his boots dangling in my view.

"Their every birth is a new disaster, Pig," Henry answers down.

Twitchy Henry calls Walbur and me "Pig" as though we were a unique creature, rather than a two-mind problem deserving of an undiscovered pronoun. This is his chief difference with Gordo, just uses our names.

"I mean, who could even keep going?" I say, "Even if they wanted to?" Walbur rooted up something crunchy. "I guess not knowing how lost they are must be of some consolation."

"Okay," says Henry, "Which one of you wants to go down there? Setting her straight won't change a thing."

Not for nothing do we follow Gordo. That's as close as we can get to being looked after. But right now Twitchy Henry will have to do.

We watch Winona go.

Winona as we knew her was the one who wove wheels from feathers and spry twigs from which she stripped the leaves by slipping them through her side teeth. She had a reedy high laugh that carried through shadow. The sound made her places all the darker when it ceased. She was easily distracted let herself be led off or else was found kneeling in the reeds, her mouth open, in supplication to nothing in particular. She was an easy encounter, available even for Fales. I had seen her with child at every harvest, but she was useless at their raising.

One Holiday I asked Winona about her wheels of cruft. Were they wards? Did they bring dreams? Rain? She could express no purpose to them beyond giggles. Between us, I think she hung them in the scrub to make it easier for the boys to find her.

I wonder if Gordo ever knew our mother.

"I don't know why it all came apart before," says Henry, doling out his words slowly. "In the old times. Or what it was like when things were still together." He gestures outward with his spear, "Whatever we've got going now is really no great shakes. Nobody is going to remember any of this."

"Who's 'we'?" growls Walbur, but he closes his eyes and drops his head as if to charge.

"Who's nobody?" I say to myself. I let the idea slide over to Walbur's head. He grunts, I hope catching a bit of my tone. Twitchy Henry probably thinks I was the one who sounded off, anyway. Twitchy Henry spits out a pellet of something that rattles down the rubble. A bone, I suppose.

When I look back, I can still see the far spot of Winona walking the other way. Winona just gave up. A wonder, really, she had come this far. Maybe if I had looked longer or harder I could have picked her up and flown her back to us, as I can sometimes do with a book which blows off the stand. But I don't know what I could have done for her thereafter. Well, nobody asked her along. If it had been just me, maybe I would have gone on down. One day I'll meet the creature who first said two heads are better than one.

We're late getting organized the day after the rising star. Kids follow us out into the thornwoods from curiosity, their love of witnessing mayhem. For all their love and concern combined would give out before they crossed the trace. We don't play music or employ any other inducement. They're not ours to keep. Gordo says we'll leave early but it almost never works out that way. He looks happy today. Yam Town must be overcrowded again. When they get to be too many, the whole place just burns down. Which is every few months. But they drag out more timber and sheets from the heaps. Yam Town can never really die. It has a kind of spirit, even though the new version never looks better than before. I'm amazed they've followed us this far. What do they know? Who knows why the kids do anything, really.

"Let's get going, Pig," says Henry. I walk us. I do us.

I never saw what Winona did with her babe. I suppose she held it to her as I've seen them do. Shoats follow along as best they can. Perhaps Walbur remembers our mother. Or who saved us from being eaten by our mother. My earliest image is of Gordo stirring a whirl of blood into my dish of salt milk. Then Gordo comes to our hole with a reed straw. Sometimes I get an image stuck in my mind so hard that everyone around me can see it, too. Our back is splitting apart from sun. We are one done sausage. At night a kind of mist descends.

Seems like more than three mornings now, since Gordo leads us past a place could scratch up a drink from the bed of the draw. I could smell it, a whole sea, waiting just below. I let

Walbur root because his tusks go out and up whereas mine go down. As such, my tusks are aces for dragging but not digging. We didn't even get down to mud. Not even close. I did the legwork until a little puddle could form in the bottom of our scrape. The dust is mostly off our back now. While working, I imagined there should be a way of counting by pain. I wish I could get a handle on days, but they just go by, one damn thing after another. I wish I could smell what's coming. But it's too hard out here. There is no time. Even back in Yam Town, it is all just one damn thing after another.

The smell of lightning woke me, out there on the wavy, failing horizon. Smelled like a dry pan scorching on the hob. Then the clouds drew up on us, in a dark pack. Twitchy Henry stooped to the only rock around. He put his palm flat to it. Right then it began to rain. His gesture seemed to split the clouds is how I hold it in memory. Great water came down, with such force, it couldn't go anywhere. The earth wouldn't take it in, so it just bounced. Torrents formed up. Fales was the first to get carried away. He had been digging a hideout in a depression. I saw him expelled at great speed by a sudden gout. New rivers needed so little time to organize themselves against us. Gordo was farther up front. I just kept my ass to the flow as best I could, put my belly down and let myself be driven like a jon boat. The storm stopped just as quickly. Once I got Walbur fully engaged—his gaze often strayed to the skies, his mouth wide for raindrops—we left the track for a long roll in the new mud. Walbur drank pure and we swole so full our new covering began to crack.

Yet another star rises from the flat horizon, like a spark from a thornwood fire, until it seems to join the Shepherd's Star. It rises straight on line to where Gordo leads, with rising speed along a shallow ellipse until it is too high for me to track. I thought again of the terrible Holiday rocket, the one resulting in the Great Yam Town Fire. How much more this one would have burned. A low, long thunder rises out and reaches us like wind but with no chill. I shivered anyway. The noise set the kids to chatter.

"Wormwood," mutters Henry.

"My dude!" exclaims a fellow with filed teeth called Ferret, who seems to have taken pride of place in Fales's absence. He has dung-dried hair and an overbite. "Broke off!" he yells, turning back to us imploring. "Was that not broke off?" His baggy knit hat flies off of its own volition, as if from the sheer excitement of its owner. Ferret's middle is grown out wrong and is poorly contained by short red pants. He thrusts his hips and draws them back. "Stick it in!" He takes a step to the right "Break it off!" Their speech—their whole culture—is so strange, like a plant so chewed over only fiber remains. Ferret waddles my way, still intoxicated by his own spectacle. "He gonna bring dastroid!" he lisps. He claps filthy hands together after every word they way they do before a fight or a fuck. I wasn't sure if he was attacking. But I turned our stern about, figuring Henry would pierce the mutant if he made a move.

Once, before this current excursion, we saved Gordo.

"Thank you, Wilbar," said Gordo.

His gratitude was misplaced, for it was on a day when Walbur had overcome me early; it was he who governed the legs. I had been regarding a green monarch emerge from its dust chrysalis, deliberating over its consumption, when Walbur set us into a charge. He laid a tear down the length of a howler's body. The beast lay in ambush of Gordo who was meandering with a weedful head.

Pulled from my reverie, I found ourselves standing over the beast as it bled out. Gordo put down his spear and did up his moccasin. The thing rolled its yellow eyes to us and gnashed its terrible teeth. We stepped back a little. "Fuck your life" woofed out Walbur. I could hear his jaw grind. "Die," he added, needlessly.

"Do wish you'd shut up, old chap," said the howler, its voice drawn taught with terrible pain. The longer I watched the beast spiral toward cold sleep, the more I forgot about monarchs. Walbur loomed over, still. We were breathing hard. He got busy sharpening his lowers against the whetters, his upper tusks.

"Going to root about in my belly, I suppose?" asked the howler with admirable aplomb. His eyes rolled back. "Go on, then," were its last words. The beast expired before the inevitable. I, Wilbar, had nodded off at the right moment. I suppose I'm comforted that my other half took over without hesitation. He, we, happened to be at the right place at the right time before the howler could leap on Gordo. I am still haunted by the notion I've underestimated Walbur. You think you know someone until the day you understand you really don't. Only Gordo could ever reliably tell us apart.

"These I must remember forever," says Twitchy Henry. "I must forever build the castle higher." Henry talks freely when his mind is flocked about. Nobody has ever seen this castle but he speaks of it as if it is a place he visits every night.

The stones here slide in the rain, sitting up slightly on the water like yams in a buttered pan. Ferret kicks a flat one and it zips away like a skatebug. Twitchy Henry lopes off to stop the stone against his foot before it can get away. He caresses it like a baby, moans, slides it back to its spot. Sandstone. Like everything in this place. Sediment.

"Wilbar."
When I'm awake we're square up to Gordo

It is no longer so stifling and my mouth tastes like water. I'm in Gordo's shadow and he's snapping his fingers at me. This, I don't like.

"What?" I say, maybe a little sharpish.

"Creep up yonder," says Gordo, patient and mysterious. Like he's about to present me with a skin of blood milk. "Have a look." Gordo wiggles his fingers in a way that means two-legged sneaking. Looking too long at Gordo inevitably puts me in mind of a world of things I don't enjoy. Thumbs. Absence from Walbur. Decent eyesight. Grace. Gordo makes me want a more maximum self, useful for all occasions. Green monarchs. What it would be like should Gordo stop bringing books and milk or else forget to let us out of the hole. Shudder to think. My best response is to stamp a trotter. Doing so made Gordo laugh so hard I resolved never to do it again. He fairly shook to stifle his amusement.

"Seriously, Wilbar," he says, "You won't believe your eyes."

I can already smell something out of the norm. I figure it will just be the kids caught in some unprecedented, awful fuck act. But I can smell something altogether more clean, an astringent odor which banishes the thought almost as soon as it arises. Piney. Gordo is still looking at me with a stupid encouraging expression on his face, motioning with his fingers. He usually starts talking by pantomiming with his fingers. It gives my brain a chance to start working on the answer before he speaks.

But he does this with everyone. He doesn't stop moving them, either, until he has said his piece. Say, if he needs five and a half of something he'll give you a look at his fingers and hold up the stub he lost to the grass whip. The five could be anything. People. Minutes. Gathered armies of howlers. The half-absent finger often uses to signify me alone, without Walbur.

Anyway. Gordo doesn't raise his voice.

What I smell cutting through the reek of the kids is men approaching. I can whiff of them without even attempting the rise. Hard to get the notion of the strangeness with the yellow molecules coming off Turgon and Erenzo's brown ones coagulating the air.

"Go on," whispers Gordo, shoving at my haunches. "Hill ain't going to climb itself."

I begin my many traverses. A big-heads pig can't just go straight up. Then it hits me on the way, the difference in the smell. "They're clean," I say down to Gordo, a few turns before the top. It is worth announcing. Clean is something I've never smelled before. Just basic men. No trace of fear or blood, no nonsense, a pure strain of them with a jaunty pine accent. Gordo puts his hands in the air and shakes his head the way he does when working up a question.

"Washed," I hiss down. "Soap. Rain. Flowers. Mild and fragrant acid. Sunshine. A wandering monarch. Where? Whence?"

The kids set to muttering, their balloon heads pressed together, their glances popping up one by one as they reach consensus.

Ferret waves about a hank of rough metal he dragged out of the waste days ago. Erenzo shifts from one club foot to the other in excitement, wheeling about to manage his eccentric equilibrium. Turgon is doubled over, coughing up blood, the way he does now and then. He seems to be clearing his lungs for action. It makes the smell of onions. This encounter is going to go south, fast. I get on up the rest of the way.

All I can make out at first is that the newcomers are four. A hand with a cut off thumb. At first, I cannot really even tally them as men. Perhaps their smell is a lie, although this would be the first time I would have been betrayed by snout. It's like the image of the galaxy in my astronomy book. Before that page, the various stars assumed no design to my eye. Thereafter, though, taking in a new page every afternoon while Walbur dozed, my night skies resolved into the order of heroes and their attendant animals.

The figure these wasteland apparitions cut is untrammeled by horrible excess variety like that of the kids, one somehow more exotic. Each wears a wide hoop around his neck. A gasket, I suppose, like on the sump hose. From hoop on up they are without hair. I couldn't even smell any wax in their ears. I get bogged down in telling this—because I don't have the straight words. The only thing obvious is that they're lost and could use some shade. They're glowing red. Little voices flock around near about them but none unwinds his scowl to speak. One of them rips one off under the bulky orange suits and my brain clicks it all into place. Onion and spices. Men. Human ones. Pure. Vegetarian. Satisfied, I return to Gordo.

"Suits" says Gordo, outlining a standing man with his fingers, "What you are seeing is suits. Why they are bigger."

"Suits for what you figure?" I ask, "Sun?" Just then, I notice Gordo's goggles are outrageous in a similar fashion, as if made by the same hand. "Against the air?"

"Astronauts," Gordo says.

"This is a bad place where we are," says Twitchy Henry, "Low on specific gravity. Wish I had a suit versus grit."

"Talk Murrican, Hank." I suggest.

"Spacemen," says Gordo. Then, slowly, to Walbur, "Men. From. Space."

"Hence," finishes Henry, "Suits."

Ferret menaces his kids into a ragged line which begins making its irregular way toward the crest. Turgon, recovered some, holds aloft a bone, his chest elaborately drenched in a livery of his own blood. He drags brother Erenzo. I don't have the right kind of eyes to see where this is going.

Walking a place where the kids have held a battle is like figuring out an Ellery Queen. Reconstitution of their outlandish and accidental violence is beyond my powers. There never seems to be any final clue. "Lernda coad," says

Walbur, which means "Get over it" their argot. I wish Walbur would read more; I fear the moment when he begins to solicit their attention. Will we be obliged to attend their parties?

Body parts, unexploded munitions, broken weapons, fires, parts, and shit lie everywhere. I'll put it all back together the best I can. They were still climbing up in their beaters' line, the filthy tide of them. I suppose they had sighted the men from space, and were just beginning to holler when a dry rippp rattled my ears and made Walbur flinch. The noise took up all the air even on our side of the ridge and downslope, beneath its wave. It kicked the air out us. We all set to coughing after it passed. All was quiet although in my mind's ear I could still hear the echo of the kids' shriek. Ferret scrabbles back over the crest, hauling the remainder of his hank of metal, brilliant white where something had sheared through it. He dropped the ruined wrench and stuck his hand between his greasy thighs. I saw the kid with tiny legs who ordinarily went about on his hands inch up after Ferret. Beeb he was called. (I have trouble with his name because my eyes never want to see him.) Beeb stood, kicking his tiny legs above, looking out from his bent little head. "My dude," he admonished me, vexed at my staring, "Lernda coad!" The kids say this in every situation where they've exceeded their psychological limits. And then, with gruesome sluggishness the tiny inverted fellow performed his final trick, sliding apart along a runny red diagonal from his hip down to his opposite shoulder. His assorted pieces tumbled down the ridge, each to their own bloody vector, leaving oily trails in the dust. The big internal pieces—a kidney?—bounced to a stop before our trotters. I can still see how the tiny soles of his torso feet had somehow remained perfectly clean, never having touched the earth, even at the last.

"Guess we better go around," sighed Gordo, ignoring Ferret who, having witnessed the end of Beeb, was now busy patting himself all over.

So we go around, keeping to the flat. We are all very humble and deliberate, Twitchy Henry, Gordo, and we. We shuffle through the dust until we can see the black scar across the reverse slope. The astro-men, oblivious, are fiddling with a box or a brick, shading their eyes from the sun. Or are shading the box, passing it around, holding it close for a look. They do not look away until Walbur clears his throat.

Here he come, croaks one of the astronauts.

They fixed on me and just laughed. I stopped worrying. If I hadn't had Twitchy Henry with his tall spear and Gordo lurking with his strange goggles they might have just cut us down. The face of the ridge, where it wasn't already black, was still on fire. High tide of the kids traced out in red. The spacemen put their big white heads back on once we were close enough for Twitchy Henry to touch them with his spear. I heard the gaskets seal. Their pink heads were now enclosed, each in a marvelous clear bubble.

They spoke in an Olden torn straight from the books. They enunciated in a sort of orderly clamor foreign to my notions of the language. Their voices were displaced from themselves. I didn't know where to look. I was very worried about seeming impolite.

Observed. Single nominal. Unknown observers. Possible redemption. Remainder Messensed-Nonsensed.

"Howdy," says Gordo. He gets by so easy behind his goggles, which make him seem stoic. Gordo snaps his fingers at the kids who follow, cackling in our long shadow. I can just take them in from my side eye. This new batch are more belted-together than usual. Yonder stands an orphan with flippers. Hither comes one on what appears to be a crutch but which later resolves to be a limb withered to the limit. Whoever assembled them did so without care. They play stupid games as they go, spitting out teeth, drawing back stumps after fair warnings. The one walking in the vanguard, just before Ferret, blinks into the light with eyes as blind as spider eggs.

The men from space do not budge.

For once, I am less worried about what Walbur might do and more about our general impression. Some of the new ones are piebald, some bear dark stains, or are spackled red. Even the spines of the ones who put up straight turn out to be fused that way, incompetent of repose. A nose too late spread across one side. An ear folded over differently than its mate, the overall effect doglike. Their most handsome, Danny Boy, is afflicted with small imbalances which trouble the legibility of his face. He is harder to read than Gordo's books about the unimaginable birds.

The kids keep extending their flanks, encouraged that they are so much more than four. They circle behind the unconcerned space men, around the old rise, shuffling through the charred remains of their brothers. At some point, this ugly hemming-in will be stopped. Only we are the ones in front this time. Me—we, particularly.

"Going to be some killing," coughs out Walbur, "Wanna split?" I can't really ever see Walbur's head, but for glimpses. Once, before still water we took each other in. That's when I noticed his tusks were up and mine were down. "Nah," I say.

They advance, their eyes to Ferret, watching for a sign to begin the rush. Mostly they're empty handed but for their comrades recovered sticks. I look over a muscle-bound kid with too much back who simply lugs a stone.

"Wilbar," says Gordo, "Go back and tell them to knock it off." Ferret has waved up a raucous howl by the time I'm halfway.

So, trotting, I hit them with the squeal. Walbur joined me, filling out the bottom. We harmonized at the pitch which would cause the most pain. Most have not heard us do this before. They stop cold, scanning for the new threat. I wish our noise were less known. Every time we use it, a little meaning gets shaved off. Once, I saw flames in the little hut Gordo knocked together down in Yam Town. It was supposed to be a school. I was using the squeal to keep them back from the Yam Farm wire then, so most everyone had already heard it. To the misbegotten school they brought bundles of brush and piled them on to stoke Gordo's unfortunate charity higher. Luckily, the kids have rolled over quite a bit since those days. We don't squeal them off the fence anymore. Thing is, the sound can cut through anything. It can stop a howler just for the time it takes Twitchy Henry's spear to complete its arc.

So, the squeal takes hold. Muscle boy lets his stone fall. A general clatter along the line installs itself as the rest follow his example. They let down all the iron and bone.

"Go on out there," says Gordo when we draw up, "I've got your back."

"I guess I'll do everything today," says Walbur. As if I were just along for the ride.

Get a load of us, cheek by jowl. Here comes pigs, one of whom says "Howdeeolalo."

Hello Go Peacetime Many Interrogative.

Listening to the space men is like reading the equation in my astronomy book. I'm not sure what I'm supposed to calculate out this mess of Olden. So I go a bit on feeling.

"They say 'I hope it isn't too late to be pals.'

They mean us, Gordo."

"Yep," he says.

"Yep goddamn what?" says Walbur.

"Help us out a little," I say in hopes of mollifying him. Gordo removes his goggles with a decisive air, the gesture of a fearless leader in search of further lucidity. I'm annoyed. I could bring the whole house down in a hot second, duck under the death beam, but the space men stand just beyond the range of my charge. "I asked you a question, Gordo."

"Tell him that's a hell of a thing to ask out here in the fields. Ask him, just between us men, where's the water."

"We men," I correct, but Gordo pretends not to hear. I twitch my ears around. The kids are inching up again. There are more here now than a moment ago. Ferret sings a children's song about dancing, illness, and decline. These kids are most certainly not alright.

"Us men," huffs Walbur.

Whole step up for green spot profile Eye Man.

"Gordo," I say, "You're up. See that box they're holding up? Go on and put your hand in there." Gordo flipped his hand over at the wrist, the way he does when thinking over what to say. Better him than we.

"Not so sure about that Wilbar," says Gordo.

"This isn't playing around now," I say.

"Nut cutting time," says Walbur, "Sun gonna stop we, fry we up. And then the kids get out the forks. Does that sound right to you? Worse.

Every howler out here already on our ass."

"What do you figure the astro-men are up to?" asks Gordo. I don't remember him ever asking my mind about anything important before.

"Dunno," I say, "Smell clean enough. Go find out."

"A part of me hesitates," says Gordo. He keeps flipping his hand and holds it high. The beauty of his ungloved hand stops the kids in their tracks. One hell of a trick, that. Would I had a hand to raise. Had I, I would keep it without blemish. Would that I were built different. Gordo holds his hand out in front of him like a gift and walks it right into the box the space man extends. They're all smiles once the object turns green. We, or Gordo anyway, are in.

FINAL JUSTICE CONFLICT NEGATIVE EVENING MEAL INTERROGATIVE.

"The yam suits don't want to rumble," I translate for Gordo. He is about to say something about the nature of the beast, going by the way he's mopping the sweat from his forehead. I cut him off before he says something primitive that might excite the kids. "'Let's get together and have a meal,' is what they're saying."

The lesser pig puts in a squeal. It passes as happiness, I suppose. Whatever happened, it didn't lead to war.

We follow the space men on down into a long ditch dug wide and straight and coffered back from collapse by such metal as I've never seen, so brilliant was its condition. Once, neat words had been painted thereupon, the letters each standing taller than Twitchy Henry. Passunder. We are moving quickly to keep up with the space men in front. They walk straight and easy, like we do once in sight of Yam Farm. I see smaller words. This Way. An arrow points against our progress. Emergency.

Inside it is cold as night and as bright as the meaning of a new word. Our trotters have never sounded bigger. The roaring echo of the sum of all our steps dissipates as the ceiling rises.The kids are struck dumb in momentary wonder. Some have never been beneath a solid roof under any circumstance. It takes me forever before I can see.

Now that we are here, wherever that is, I cannot think of anything but return. We came through a wire. They warned us. Olden uses the same words for death as we use today. The kid with a globby yoke of muscle across his shoulders cannot resist. His fingers sizzled off neat to the line where the wire kissed them. He does not bleed, cries mostly of surprise. Lumpy simply beholds his hand. The air smells wrong but Ferret, giggling picks up the fingers, puts them into the pocket where he keeps lizards and roots.

This wire worries me fierce. One of the spacemen held it up for me when it was my turn to go under. I cannot imagine how I will be able to cross it alone. Dig, I thought. But digging here would be such hard going. We'll need at least Gordo wearing his goggles just to see the damn thing.

The spacemen let their suits down into little piles from which they step. Underneath their clothing is the same yam color. They smell no different than before. A hard animal slid to us, smelling of lightning, and removed the suits. Then, it was a lot of lights, voices, and people coming and going. I felt like the first time I saw Gordo turn the donkey engine over. My eyes could not take in the wheel and the steam or how one agitated the other. I had to read a book or two before I could make it out in detail or even imagine its insides.

It does smell delicious inside. A light goes on over a long, laden table. Women come. They put down trays. It takes a fair amount of walking under the dome just to get there. Gordo's hands have become a flock of sparrows, each carrying a different message. "Where did this heavy table come from?" he says, "I mean this harvest table? It's the middle of summer. Have you ever seen such food?"

Regular tribute truck farm clockwork venus home special ship glucose proteins lipids automated slaughter automated landing.

Gordo stops and stares me down, his hands spread in supplication.

"They say they have a squared-away farm up in Venus City," I say, "They won't say where Venus City is. Maybe space. Or they're lying. Rest assured, it is a hell of a long way. The real nature of any of these tales? The space dudes won't say." Sometimes to convince Gordo, I try to use all the words and then some. Which usually makes him frown and redirect.

"Chow's on," I tell Gordo, "They say to eat up."

There is even a place for me at the table. I can just see over the edge. Walbur pulls, frantic to get at the tasty, steaming piles. Whatever it is, I want it inside of our body as soon and as fast as possible. But I can't get my feet up there without overturning the whole setup. The diplomacy of the space men has hard physical limits, apparently. A space woman notices our quandary approaches me with a useless stool.

A word about the space women. I think it must be their hair. The smell of it could change the alignment of your entire being toward the better, skip you right over the shadow of any neutral moral state. It made me want to plow out the hardscrabble at Yam Farm immediately, increase our yield while bathed in light, find a lady pig with white shoulders. Every space creature had two good-looking friends and so on back to infinity. While under their dome I am never subject to the same allure twice. Beast I may be, but I do have a snout. Their effect, the women's, on the kids is like when Skaggs first made a red cloud hover above a crowd of children with his flamer. They are bound, ardent. I have never seen the kids so dumbstruck.

Ferret recovers first. "Just chunk it all on the floor, darling," he says, "Pig don't sit." She was standing on the Walbur side of me otherwise

I must have said it myself. There is no making oneself heard once Walbur's excitement takes hold. Food unhinges him. "No worries!" shouts Ferret, encouraging a brunette who smells like an apple tree in bloom, "Like they do at home. Seriously, dude. Dump it!" She hesitates yet.

"It's okay," says Gordo evenly. "Floor is how we do them back home."

The apple maid places the tray down with quiet grace, startling away after Walbur puts a surge into our legs, upsetting the whole deal so the meal ends up disorganized and dispersed.

"Sooo-eeee!" puts in Joyz. Until that moment I thought Joyz had been sawn in two or something. All the other kids are busy eating. Even Twitchy Henry doesn't bother with this joke any longer. With the kids someone is always watching, ready to mock every misstep. Walbur fills our gut. I'm free to speak.

"Like you never ate off the deck, Joyz," I retort. The apple maid laughs. Her laugh would be like the sound of Yam Farm Trace if the trace ran clear. A small, hard animal smelling of fire and abomination slides up and spins some blue brushes at me.

I grunt it off. "Fuck away from my food."

The floor scatter we're tucked into tastes of yams, meat, and wild onions in high summer. It tastes like everything that I have not yet tasted, like every color. This is the taste of the world as it was before the moon turned green. Maybe roast turkey, too, and sugar pudding. Even the floor has a savor different from any other floor I've known. The closest candidate would be a salty lick of clay. But sweet at the same time. The floor tastes like Holiday. Point is, nothing is reminiscent of parts put through the grinder.

Half of Ferret's pals are still lost in the comings and goings of the maids and the other half are snouted into their bowls and cups. They are getting a little crocked. The hard animal comes and goes, brushing up their pink and yellow indiscretions. It looks as if, lately, they've been subsisting mostly on sand spiders. Lumpy, with his newly-mauled hand looks up, wide eyed. He uses the member to make a crippled version of a courtly gesture to a stately blonde. Once the awful moment draws to a confused conclusion, resulting in the blonde's awkward withdrawal, I realize Lumpy is aping Skaggs when he makes a speech from the Yam Town low-water bridge. Walbur fills the air with sharp squeals. That's his laughter. He sounds years younger than me, a piglet. Our stomach is a hard fist of energy and gas. Lumpy withdraws his horrible hand, taken aback by its effect. Because of the limb there can be no conclusion. Usually, I close my eyes and wait until Walbur stops. I keep thinking that, since we share the same stomach, maybe he'll learn from me, hold his peace. Enough is enough. I try to flip the notion over to him, but he's not receiving. The spacemen stir. They look a bit nervy. It dawned on me that they might be able to whip a wire across the whole room. I don't expect our low stature would save us.

I don't quite remember the corner they gave us to sleep. A wide and cool place like everywhere. The sharpness of our smelly invasion is striking, requiring much forgiveness. This was my last thought before finding myself in a dream. I was walking just beyond the arch. The vision of the green sow with the white band came to me. She was rooting in the desert. She wasn't going to find anything. I knew this like you know things in dreams. I had it in mind to wander over and warn her about the wire.

Walbur, in my dreams is a mute weight. Sometimes he is absent from my body, yet I feel his weight anyhow. How there's always something more to tell in a dream and why it might be better not to start. How worried I was about the wire. There was also the vague sense of promise glowing out from the green sow that she would turn her haunches for me. But, first, we were to do it on more humid ground. I walked on until I felt something pull me at the withers. I started forward, hard against it, as when pulling a kill-laden travois. When it became more difficult to bear, I did a fancy turn to square up on whatever it might have been. There lay a large head. Walbur, going by the spot on the inside ear. I realize my side-eye is empty of the familiar shadow and blur. I startle awake, thirsty, and small-hours horny.

I'm up before Walbur. I watch my brother from my inside eye. As he comes around I twitch our legs first. They are to be mine all day.

"Wilbar," he says, "Let us stay here." Some mornings he tries to speak more. And better.

Before his brain gets clouded by the day. "We could eat more. Get stronger." This is the first time we've slept indoors with regular folk, with Gordo and Twitchy Henry. Walbur's articulation is so bad. I am the only one who can make him out reliably. His talking embarrasses me. He's heard me tell him to shut up so many times. Over the night, I did our best with respect to farts. The men from space must have some kind of system to help with smells. We are still perched on a wonderful cloud, and a salty floor cool as mud. Thing is, though, I need to find a door. My morning need is heavy and will not wait.

"Gordo."

But Gordo is elsewhere. What I get instead is Ferret.

"Hooo, pig," he declares, showing off his pointy teeth, "Lemme sleep."

"Gordo," I say, "Get him."

"Where's Gordo?" he repeats, mimicking Walbur's dull, huffy voice. Ferret giggles through his nose, the way he always does before saying something he will have to reel back. "Who am I talking to?"

"You mean 'Whom', retard." I say.

Nobody is showing me the way toward a wallow. A spotlight follows me wherever I go. A warm voice comes over everything.

Negative impolite defecation protocol proceed increase biomass.

Everyone watches. I am getting away from myself. I dump large where I stand. It is terrible and fast, beneath words. I almost apologize. But what would be the point? I wander back under the table to hide from the spotlight once the shameful moment is over. We are, after all, under a dome too wide to see the limit. They have a system for the light. They have a system for everything. That's the deal. The hard animal aspirates my pile and leaves behind the smell of honeysuckle in rain. I watch from beneath the table. Ruefully is the word. What I hear is the kids snoring. And beyond that, sighing. And Gordo's happy laugh. My beastly excess has been erased as surely as the white ash that falls to signal the start of hunting season, how it curls and disappears. We bed back down on the warm square where the floor is soft. For now this is our favorite place. We are warm in the right places, cool in others.

"I'll do a lot of things, but I won't do that!" Gordo's voice is clear and general above the sighs. I cannot smell my way to him. The dome makes hearing easy and important. There is some stress in his saying, but some delight as well. Some play. I remember, long ago, trying to step away from Walbur, before I understood. Boy, Gordo laughed at us as we wiggled out our first, pinched circle. Gordo resolved our existential dilemma by setting his arms to either side of us so there was no way but forward into the wilds and everything that might mean. Maybe it would be to the good.

How tiny we once were.

There's nothing to do now but hold to our spot on the floor and let Walbur sleep.

A relief, actually.

"Okay Walbur," says Gordo, "I don't mean to say it hasn't been real."

We're standing in the portico of the dome, where the last shadow lay between the space-men and the day. My bags are heavier than they ever have been. I suspect Ferret is using me to pack out silverware. The finality in Gordo's voice banishes any further thought of Ferret.

"Gordo, you're going to have to practice talking to children," I say, "You're talking to my stupid head. Your message isn't getting through."

"Nooo," lows Walbur, "Nooo." Sometimes, I admit, he gets Gordo's drift long before I do. As with howlers. As now, with this most unwelcome departure.

"I guess we'll leave it to you, old buddy," says Gordo.

"You always do," I say, although this is not the truth and we both know it. It, whatever—everything—has always been left to someone else. Up until now. "And who the hell is this 'we' you speak of?"

Gordo removes his goggles, straps them out for wider fit, slaps them over my head. My eyes settle at the edges of the lenses. At once I see we are in a thicket of sharp lines glowing across our way. Had the world's dangers always appeared to him so clearly as Gordo steered us?

"Tell Henry if it gets to be too much," he says, "But, for now, use my spectacles to get beyond the wire."

Walbur is rubbing his head against Gordo's leg. Gordo talks above his disordered caterwaul.

"I'm going up to Venus," says Gordo. His finger traces a long, shallow arc. Addressing me, I suppose. "Beyond the moon."

"I can smell Yam Farm from here, Gordo."

"The kids will follow you. Or they won't. It doesn't matter whether you get them through or not. Don't be sidetracked by their fates. They can only get you killed." Gordo's filling the air and the time and will keep doing so until I end it. "Mind the chasing walls. They'll close you in."

"Remember, Gordo," I said.

"What's that?" he said, seeming happy that I'd hit the ball back over.

"Wherever you go, there you are."

He doesn't have an answer, shrugs his shoulders.

"Never die, Gordo."

"Okay Pig," he says.

"What about us?" I say.

Gordo kneels down to my level. I can see myself reflected in his eyes. "Root hog or die," he says.

Maybe Walbur looked back. I didn't have it in me.

❁

The wires, shining green, sang in the breeze, hung thicker than I had imagined. There is no straight way out, no message to read in their lattice. I don't imagine we would have ever made it through following my nose. Nor had I ever imagined how narrow our previous path had been. I could see the way out from under the portico and up the crater wall, all the way to where the noise and light began. We would walk between. We would lead.

"I'm so sick of goodbyes," says Walbur a little down the line. We're alone so nobody can hear his smeared, unacceptable speech. When had Walbur become friends with Fales? I keep my nose to the wind. I don't let on how surprised I am that he notices. Somehow, Twitchy Henry is standing on the other side of the wires, waiting, knocking out his pipe.

At the head of a cavalcade of mutants trotted a bow-heavy pig. They follow this beast up and out of a coffered tunnel mouth until they are again on the hard pan. The Shepherd's Star rises behind them. All but the pig raise their eyes to it in wonder. A laden sledge floats on the low air, is ridden by a tall man with a spear across his knees. Or so the report of the howler scout would go. Our spoor cannot be hard to follow. Like Gordo, I have always prized being ahead when the going seems sure. It is me now who steers us all. The kids do as best they can with the wires. A few still fell apart in halves, surprised by mid-stride bisection when after straying across a wire. There's no knowing what tempts them from the path I set. There's no knowing, really, how far and narrow we will have to walk.

The kids simply cannot keep themselves from investigating the little piles of bones that line on the wrong side. The moment anything catches their eye they forget every admonition. Reaching for a blowing piece of cloth and the arm drops into the dust. "Just put one foot in front of the other," I tell a kid on scrub wood crutches, "Pass it on." The muscle hump, Lumpy, fished back what looked like a pistol from a burnt pile with his good hand. I heard the weapon's sharp report behind me, quickly followed by the customary levity which breaks out among accident witnesses. Through the goggles, the wires run lower until they descend into the earth. Their glow is strong enough that it follows them a little way below the dust. I turn them to the stars. Large disks which I have never heretofore seen traverse the skies with a slow majesty. I wonder who or what rides within them.

"Let's go," I say once the laughter, medical attention, and horseplay seem to have died down.

"No," Twitchy Henry says.

"I don't see anything ahead," I say, "We're clear. We're moving out."

"Don't recognize these rocks," says Twitchy Henry, "Ain't moving until I do."

"Slip these goggles off my eyes," I ask. He

does it but does not otherwise budge. I can tell he's cross, for even having to avert his gaze from the waste momentarily, tear his eyes away from the noise, his mind off on a memorized arrangement of farther stones.

"It's been real, Henry," I say.

We, whoever else has the strength to follow, shuffle on.

We find their strange bones in the brush everywhere I've ever been. Except the dome. I navigate by distant glimmers of white and root about upon arrival. What you would take to be the delicate arcs of jumper horns turn out to be fused into a mannish skull. The kids just crunch on through them but some demon inside Walbur drives him to fight me for the legs so to draw near, sniff. I steer us off from a low stone wall. I wonder if some future passerby, coming upon our own bones, of me, and Twitchy Henry, would mark us as any different from the kids, another curiosity off the main branch of evolution. The howlers, their scent ever on the wind, tempting distance, ever at the edges, snap me back to leadership.

At the next outcrop, just at midday—the eminence looked like a ship being dragged below the sand by its stern—out stepped Henry from a sharp slice of black shade.

"Come and see," he said. I waddle over to where he squats with his tall spear. The sands fall to a smallish cave.

Standing inside, Walbur roots at some little,

huddled form. He gets a little bit of it off. I walk us back quickly as soon as I discern its spine, its tiny teeth. Every vertebra arranged into a fine arc of holy perfection. The creature had been not much larger than a lizard.

"Baby love," moaned Walbur. I'm not sure anyone else heard. I don't know anyone, save Gordo, who might care if he did.

"Smells she," says Walbur, "I mean Winona".

I reproached myself for imagining that he had been gnawing the remains. I don't have a clear view of Walbur; I'm give in to the lowest of expectations, sometimes.

I swim us back up the sand, more strength than grace, and head over to a peninsula of the ship rock's shadow where I might have some perspective on the wastes and noise. At best, Winona's was an effort to keep the howlers back, to lead them away from us. The realization is as scorching as the encroaching sun. The shadow wheels away from us. The floating sled of space food awaits delivery to Yam Town. I could just walk away. Yam Town would starve. I would starve. It is past time to move.

The howlers growl nearer. This owes to the narrowing of the walls. We did not appreciate them until what we took to be simple piles of field stone rose above the creosote. They are now higher than Twitchy Henry's shoulder, expertly arranged by some historical genius. To be completely fair to myself, the kids reported nothing. Maybe some scaled over early. Now I can hear them calling from the wrong side of the walls, from both sides. They call to be helped over, but that just brings the howlers nearer. Last night, we heard Bruto being ripped apart. It was a long business. We didn't fall asleep until just before dawn. Strange how it is far easier to shake a leg when there are people at your back, expecting you to rise, even if they are driven chiefly by hunger and boners.

The walls are too high for the sled to cross. Turgon and Erenzo argue and fiddle, but cannot find the control. They only succeed in making the contraption float lower. We go on because that's what I decide.

The walls narrow. Sometimes Twitchy Henry rides the sledge. "We've overshot," he says. But mostly he stays. In his absence it is Ferret who rides. I am taunted always but less when I am well in front. I would be happy to have an array of fools before me, as when Gordo was around. To my surprise Turgon drags Erenzo ahead to scout upon my suggestion. They leave a trail of space food wrappers smeared with their own waste. I wonder what other task with which they might be entrusted. At some point, we're going to have to clever the sled over the wall. And somebody will have to lift me, too. So my outing with the kids continues.

❋

It emerges in the afternoon from behind a creosote thicket. Not man, nor animal, nor smart-ass admixture. Not a howler but a jagware, the first I've seen, bold as brass. In ferocity, it doesn't come up to the beast I had made in my mind. It smelled and was hairy, stooped and was low-moving and whatever else I am not far-sighted enough to say. It was supple and it bore the odor of murder and domination and had an air as if it had never known confinement. A jagware looks like a cloud of sand flies dialed one shade darker. It moves a step or three faster than I can follow. It pants away heat from open jaws. Only then could I spot it easily by its red maw. But what of Gordo's goggles? One might well ask. Useless, hanging around my neck. The goggles, this time, they did nothing.

"Twitchy Henry?" I called.

But who's left is Erenzo.

"Titchy Enree," he wheezes. His mimic makes me sound whinier than I am. We glare. He remained perched up on the sled. "And I ain't climbing down, Pig. No how, no way."

I have no ready method of shaming him to get what I want. My only out is to run back to where the walls are low while the rest are being killed. And through the night. And through the morning beyond.

While I was contemplating escape, the jagware emerges and drags down Danny Boy by the head. The thing's lower incisors punch through the tops of his eye sockets.

All the play is drains from Danny's limbs. My mind slips and my legs start to move. There is some innate cunning bred into me, a secret even from myself. His name is Walbur. The jagware is busy shaking Danny, making his legs dance. Walbur takes us downwind, turning on the forelegs, for all the world like Gordo making the kerosene tractor pirouette by standing on one brake. A spray of Danny's blood falls warmly on our back. The jagware's tail is raised in effort, revealing a filthy star. We cross the invisible line where my vision reddens and our genuine charge begins. The rest is flashes and dust and wet stuff across my face. The first thing I can make out clearly once my vision clears is the jagware's blood trail. It is easy to see, as it smells so badly. Its blood is a wide turnpike of fear leading into the brush.

We come up on Danny, abandoned. He lies face down. He stands bleeding in spurts from the holes above his eye sockets, just like a horn lizard. He points toward the spot where the howler has gone over the wall, over a sort of rude stair that might have otherwise passed unremarked, save for its dark path of ichor. Danny Boy strides to the wall with the air of wanting to continue their exchange of views. As if he were after justice.

"Thanks pigs," Danny says over his shoulder. We watch him go with the blood still jumping out of his head. He stops at the top, wipes his eyes clear. "Elite only!" he exclaims before the remaining kids. Then he steps off the wall to whatever waits on the other side.

A day later.

"Give it up," says Walbur.

"I'm going to be the one who didn't give up," I say, "You just enjoy the ride." It feels good hollering in harmony with my stupid head for once. It feels stupid, but also strong. We can't walk over. The sled won't float over, either. The thing just bumps softly against the obstacle like a jon boat at the pier. Ferret hops down and pushes hard, hoping maybe to displace the wall, an irregular stone. No dice. The closer the sled gets to the wall, the harder it is to push. We've got maybe an hour of daylight left. Everything is lit in red. I let Walbur wheel us around from time to time, ready for a charge. The other kids keep off, or cross over, or are otherwise still. Turgon, his pack laden with space food, steps off the sled and onto the wall. The craft dips in the air under his push. He grips fast to Erenzo. Together, hand in hand they leap from sight. Just when I've decided I've been left to what is now exclusively my own floating device, Danny appears upon the wall. His spindly arms hang down to me. I notice that Danny's face seems brighter for the brass screws stopping the holes in his head.

The kid pulls at the stone, I suppose bracing his legs farther down. The capstone comes away with him. A heartbeat later, the wall itself crumbles away. Danny hurries a handful of kids who stoop and clear the rubble. The sled floats over with ease. As do I step.

Danny survives over the next days, walking just behind me for most of the way, whistling now and then, as if he were now responsible for me. One day, we leave him at an outcrop Henry knew, propped up in the shade.

"Dafuk?" Twitchy Henry asks me, touching his eyebrows, meaning the screws in Danny's head.

"I don't know what to say so that you would believe," I answer. "He deserves to rest."

"Alright," says Twitchy Henry.

Skaggs ended up with the sled. He scooted himself around town and across the draw, dangling one leg over to push it forward or digging his heel in to stop when he wanted to yell at me to get out of the way. He even made his Holiday speech perched atop it, beneath a cold clear sky full of stars, pure of the moon. My hope was that the magic in the sled would last into hunting season proper so as to relieve me of the meat bags, but one morning the device settled down for good outside Skaggs's hole and could not be coaxed to rise again. More kids made it through the winter than usual, thanks to the space food, though I barely enjoyed a lick of it. I still find the silver food paper on the wind, throughout the bushes, dancing amid the bones. I figure Ferret must be out there, in a fresh-dug scrape, living off his stock. He'll be along. Or he won't. Or maybe Danny Boy will. Either way. Any way. Nothing surprises me. Except we're still here. All of us, however whole, under Gordo's Star.

STARSHIP

Jeffro Johnson

The primordial "mazey dungeons" of the original *Dungeons & Dragons* game bear little resemblance to the adventure modules which would ultimately set the tone for fantasy role-playing. In the first place, they didn't have to make sense. More baffling was the absence of anything resembling either a story, a narrative arc, or even a broad- brush adventure scenario. The old rules simply encouraged the referee to produce a game environment so large as to be effectively endless.

The gap between this earlier style of play and that which was derived from the later adventure modules is best illustrated by the elusiveness of the game's most notorious dungeon complexes. According to the third volume of the original D&D booklets, Gary Gygax's Greyhawk campaign contained at least thirty levels and was still growing. Greyhawk was neither a setting nor a brand. It was a mega-dungeon and not much else. It was also unlike anything that would ever be published for the game, having "over a dozen levels in succession downwards, more than that number branching from these, and not less than two new levels under construction at any given time." Its contents were completely off the wall, spanning " a museum from another age, an underground lake, a series of caverns filled with giant fungi, a bowling alley for 20' high giants, an arena of evil, crypts," and more.

Referees smitten with the charm of the original game would naturally pay good money to get a look at Greyhawk. But when TSR released the first D&D supplement under that name, they were only teasing. The supplement does purport to detail inside information directly from "the devious minds behind Greyhawk Castle." But its contents amount to little more than a grab bag of rules elaborations: the thief class, half-elves, to-hit and damage bonuses for fighters with high unmodified strength scores, hit dice bonuses for high constitution scores, the use of differing polyhedral dice both for each class's hit die and also for varying the damage done by each weapon type and more. It's hard now to imagine playing D&D at all without these signature rules, but Greyhawk contains almost no information at all about the sprawling dungeon complex that was their proving ground!

The *World of Greyhawk* boxed set for the AD&D game would later detail more than anyone would want to know about a fantasy setting: lands, peoples, kingdoms, pantheons—even names for the months and the days of the week. It's a ponderous almanac for a world that doesn't exist. And yet information about Greyhawk castle is again mentioned only in passing. Adding insult to this unsatisfactory state of affairs, TSR released a product called "Castle Greyhawk" in 1988, following Gygax's departure from the company. While it features a modestly-sized dungeon spanning a dozen levels, each one was a gag level penned by a completely different author who had nothing to do with the original campaign. "Castle Greyhawk" bore absolutely no resemblance to the legendary Greyhawk castle.

Piecing together what that early Gygaxian campaign was really like is a task that's been left to historians and dedicated grognards to sort out. And that is just as well. The core premise of the original D&D rules pamphlets was that the dungeon master would devise his own monster-sized dungeon and not just play around with someone else's campaign. (As the afterword of the original rules booklets states, "why have us do any more of your imagining for you?") Such an undertaking is so foreign to subsequent incarnations of the game, and so beyond the scope of most peoples' tabletop experiences, that it would be nice if we had something closer to a worked example of how to game that way—if only to confirm that it could be done and that it really was once the default way to role play.

Fortunately, we have just such a thing. It just happens to not be a D&D product at all. Instead, it's a science fiction role-playing game. The very first one, no less! *Metamorphosis Alpha* was the brain child of James Ward. He not only knew Gygax personally and gamed with him, but he was also ordained by him to undertake the project. The stamp of authentic old school role-playing reads in bold relief upon every bit of the game.

Unlike later science fiction games which would include intricate rules for building worlds and starships and travelling the universe, *Metamorphosis Alpha* starts its players as primitive tribal people deep inside the bowels of the starship *Warden*, a tremendous generation ship that's in dire straits after flying too close to a radiation cloud. For James Ward, the huge dungeon complex was so intrinsic to the premise of role-playing, such an edifice would remain a fundamental element of even a science fiction variant. He also took for granted the idea that you would draw up your own plans—this time for a tremendous starship fifty miles across and seventeen levels deep.

The best thing about this book is that it actually makes such an undertaking seem like something within reach of mere mortals. The side view of the Warden's seventeen levels is the sort of amateurish sketch that anyone could manage—and they are just stacked on top of one another. The absence of any sublevels branching off in random directions is its most obvious deficiency, but the message is clear all the same: you don't have to be an artist in order to pull this off. Thumbnail sketches are provided to go along with each level's capsule description, something that could be quickly dashed together on a single sheet of scratch paper. Impeccable production standards are simply not a prerequisite for this undertaking.

As a model for the referee, two levels are given a more in-depth treatment. One is a complete layout and description of the city level, something typically left as an exercise for the referee in other early gaming materials. It isn't stocked with creatures and encounters, so the breakdown of the forest level is far more instructive. The second sample level is a fully-keyed hex map detailing an oval deck forty-nine miles across and twenty-four miles wide in the style of a D&D wilderness area. The entries are terse, enumerating little beyond what creatures live where and what equipment they have. The design ethic employed here presages the "one-page dungeon" approach to adventure design that would be rediscovered by the Old School Renaissance decades later. Adhere to it and you will craft dungeons that are both easy to create and referee!

Though that sample deck remains state of the art to this day, not everyone was able to fully appreciate it at the time. According to the designer in a 1978 article for *The Dungeoneer,* Ward was frequently asked at conventions how he made his levels. To address this, he provides there another fully playable starship *Warden* level, this time based on a hunting and fishing wilderness gone wild. Yet again he steers novice referees away from the sort of foolish consistencies irrelevant to real gaming. He encourages them to not get hung up on how the overall proportions of the levels impact the exterior shape of the ship—indeed, this level is square in order to extract the most value from a sheet of hex paper!

This new starship level is otherwise in line with the forest level presented in the original rules. The sole exception is it bakes an ongoing conflict between mutants and androids into the location descriptions. That evolving status between factions on the various starship decks is something Ward would touch on in other magazine articles shortly after the game's release. Besides a large number of additional creatures, it is the one thing that he most felt needed additional elaboration for the game to really make sense. Such efforts would have to wait, as TSR opted to retire the game in favor of the much weirder *Gamma World* (also by Ward.) *Metamorphosis Alpha* faded into obscurity. With the possible exception of TSR's AD&D module *Expedition to Barrier Peaks,* the concept of space-themed mega-dungeons vanished from the hobby.

From the vantage point of a *Gamma World* fan looking back, the most surprising thing about *Metamorphosis Alpha* is that it is a rather earnest attempt at a serious science fiction game. For one thing, there's no silliness like a rollerball trophy, tuba, or microwave oven on the d100 treasure lists. Every item has a purpose, significant gameplay value, and is consistent with the game's overall vision. The robots and androids that come off as a particularly baffling setting element in the later game suddenly make perfect sense. They, and everything else, are fully explained and are given a cogent rationale for being where they are and behaving the way that they do. Unlike D&D, *Tunnels & Trolls*, and *Traveller*, *Metamorphosis Alpha* is not a hot mess of multiple and incompatible paperback series arbitrarily stitched together. To create this game, James Ward hewed very closely to a single literary antecedent: Brian Aldiss's novel *Starship*. For harried referees who don't quite know where to begin, an understanding of just how the game departs from its primary source can make all the difference.

The elongated egg shape of Aldiss's starship is a dead match for the *Warden*. The incredible scope of its eighty-four coin-shaped decks is its defining feature. Instead of stacking one ovoid deck on top of the other top to bottom, they are strung together as circles from front to back. Every deck of the ship connects via a main corridor running from bow to stern through its longitudinal axis. Perhaps the biggest difference of all is that the ship is returning to earth with little more than a skeleton crew suffering from mutational side effects after taking on contaminated water. In contrast to this, the *Warden* is fully loaded, its accident occurring en route to the colony world.

Aldiss's survivors are so reduced that they find it difficult to believe that they are on a starship "thick with phantoms and riddles and mysteries and pain." As far as they are concerned, the world consists of nothing else but an endless series of rooms and passages thick with a "ponics" plant that sprawls everywhere, growing into the ship's metal walls. The protagonist's call to adventure is triggered by the discovery of a complete deck plan of the starship—something that James Ward necessarily excluded from his game. (Mapping out the unknown is half the fun, after all.) Where Aldiss allows his protagonist to acquire a diary explaining how everything came to be the way it was, Ward supposes a central computer that can be used to drive play by doling out a series of quests that could potentially culminate in the ship correcting its course.

The various factions of Aldiss's *Starship* map fairly well to those of *Metamorphosis Alpha*. First of all, there are the mysterious giants who appear to have created everything for an unknown purpose only to later vanish. Then there are the various tribes of humanity, some living in the more civilized region known as Forwards, others living in varying degrees of desperation and primitivity. Right in line with rules that allow pure strain humans to amass large numbers of mutated followers, there is a renegade human that has gained a following of mutant humanoids all exiled from their tribes due to their deformities. The insidious Outsiders infiltrate the tribes, spying on them and manipulating them for their own ends in much as do *Metamorphosis Alpha*'s androids. Finally, baffling hyper-intelligent rats prowl the air ducts and underdecks, wielding legions of moth and rabbit minions to their own inscrutable ends.

Though James Ward retains the broad strokes of each of Aldiss's *Starship* factions, he has no problem introducing many more mutant animal types, including humanoids that mutated from animal types such as the Wolfoid, the Bearoid, and the Cougaroid. (While out of place in contemporary po-faced science fiction settings, these creatures are way too much fun to not take to excess at the tabletop.) In his sample starship levels, he reproduces the factional breakdown of Aldiss's ship in microcosm, allowing the fate of each level to adopt its own direction in response to the players' actions. This is one reason why James Ward was so confident in his abilities to quickly work up seventeen irradiated starship levels ex nihilo while many of the game's purchasers floundered. True, Ward was initiated into the hobby by one of the architects of fantasy role playing. The campaign he participated in with Gygax was one in which anything could happen, too. But he also had a fully-realized generation ship to prime his imagination and give him a starting point for his own creations. The basic premise of dropping the players into a dynamic multi-sided conflict would stand the test of time as well: Gygax himself would later select this very scenario as the proving ground for new players and referees picking up their copy of Basic D&D for the first time in the module *The Keep on the Borderlands*.

Equipped with these inspirations, you can bring this old game to life as effortlessly as James Ward. Whether you're looking to unlock the mysteries of Greyhawk Castle or *Gamma World*, you'll find the answers you seek in *Metamorphosis Alpha*. Whether your players are adventuring on a ghostly generation ship or in the depts of a sprawling dungeon complex, there should be something in Brian Aldiss's *Starship* to get you on track.

If you make one change to your gaming, though, do this: Make it big! Doing so was not merely an idiosyncrasy of old school play; it was foundational. It forces referees to adopt a healthy minimal ethic just to get things off the ground. This fosters both independence and a mastery of the game, buttressed by a unique anti-fragility. On the players' side there is no hint anywhere of what they are "supposed" to do. There is no script. There are no explicit victory conditions.

In the face of a truly large mega-dungeon, the joy of exploration takes center stage. Here, the real value of the simplistic and easily dashed-off dungeon keys become evident. It becomes that much easier for the dungeon environment to be altered in response to player action, making the desire for a worthy quest possible. Embrace this design ethic and you will not only achieve role-playing enlightenment—you will also never need another splat book again. You will finally be able to deliver a tabletop role-playing experience where the players really can go anywhere and do anything they might imagine.

THE JUDGMENT OF DAGANHA

Schuyler Hernstrom

The great highway stretched out before them. The miles flew underneath the wheels of the iron horse as they rode. Mortu the Kinslayer, Mortu the Merciful, scion of the north, where warriors were once bred like princes breed their race horses. Kyrus the Wise, a man of faith, of sacred vows and probing intellect, sharp tongued and sure of himself. Sometimes too much so, as a conflict with an evil sorcerer has resulted in his imprisonment in the body of a small monkey. Our heroes cross the wasteland in search of a cure for Kyrus, seeking magics and wisdom from the east.

Mortu rode with the throttle wide open. The steed rumbled between his legs as the hot wind played with the long locks of his dark hair. To either side was desert of wide plains broken occasionally by low hills, covered in a haze of heat and ochre dust. His mouth was turned at the corners as he revved the heart of the steel beast.

Kyrus regarded him and yelled over the din. "You are more sullen than usual, my heathen friend."

Mortu's weather-beaten face showed concern as he replied. "Don't you hear that? The heart of the beast skips a beat and labors more than usual."

"It seems the same deafening racket to me."

"No. The beast grows ill. If I don't see to it we could have trouble later."

Kyrus scratched his furry chin. "If I am reckoning correctly, we are about ten leagues from a road that leads south, all the way to Kwarzim, a city on the southern edge of the waste, fabled for its riches. A caravanserai should mark the exit."

Mortu smirked, "You remember this from one of your books?"

"Indeed I do, and my memory is infallible."

"Do you remember the time you caused us to be lost just outside of Bursan?"

"I do not."

With no better idea Mortu held his course. After a time, a complex of low domes rose from the horizon. Above them was a graceful tower, perhaps thirty feet tall. It was gently curved and marked with odd lines, an alien relic left from the long departed Illilissy. Next to the complex Mortu saw a tract leading from the road. He brought the steed to a halt and inspected the rough road. The highway was a wide black strip. The road before him was not much more than a beaten track.

"This must be it. Here caravans from the west rest a night before making for Kwarzim." With that Kyrus hopped off Mortu's shoulder onto the dusty ground and made a great show of stretching his cramped limbs.

The caravanserai was empty of other travellers. The domes were arranged in a U shape around a tiled courtyard. The alien tower stood at the north corner. A tall, narrow doorway led inside each of the odd domiciles. Kyrus regarded the first. On its sun-beaten side was a line of text, crudely written in charcoal. The barbarian stood beside him. "What does it say?" It was a scrawling script, written boldly.

Kyrus puzzled at it. "Hmm. This is a script associated with the Arazi. It has distant roots in common with our own Imperial but has undergone many changes over the centuries. Interpretation is made difficult by their habit of not including short vowels." The monkey's brow furrowed as he pondered. He continued, "This word here, likely it means 'beware', then a descriptor, 'giant', something bad, evil, predatory, a sense of imminence, urgency, with connotations of impurity and waywardness." He turned to Mortu. "This is encouraging. These people warn each other against evil, against impurity and its concomitant dangers. Perhaps they are a pious folk." He scratched his tiny chin. "Curious. Oliverio's Encyclopedia paints the Arazi in a wholly different light. He reported the people there as rather venal, appeasing their dark gods of the waste with bloody sacrifice. Perhaps some Nestor has beaten me there."

Mortu pushed the steed to the edge of the courtyard and dismounted. He washed at a water pump, cleansing his face and bare torso of the grime of the road. He drank his fill of the cool liquid, tasting faintly of the deep minerals from whence it came.

Kyrus made a noise of triumph from the dimness of a dome and emerged dragging a discarded pot behind him. With Mortu's help the vessel was filled with cool water and the monk was soon escaping the heat in his ersatz bath. The barbarian knelt by his steed and unrolled his tool pouch. His abilities were limited more by a lack of parts than expertise. The iron steed was a tool of war for his people and all the men of his tribe were trained in its care and workings. He peered at the heart where it sat under the tear drop shaped vessel that held energy. It was practically limitless, an invention of the long-departed Illilissy. Mortu debated pulling the heart apart to clean its innards. The proposition was risky. Damage might be exacerbated and the pair would be left stranded until a caravan came. Then, likely, a long search for parts before resuming their quest on the iron steed.

He started the beast's heart and squatted low to listen to the rumbling idle.

Kyrus leaned back with his arms around the rim of the pot. He turned to his friend.

"Might we have a moment's quiet before starting that accursed alien machine again?"

Kyrus eyes grew wide and he screamed, a high pitched, squeaking sound. He flung himself from his bath and waved his hands furiously toward Mortu.

Behind the barbarian the scorpion lifted his tail. It rose, half again as tall as Mortu, bulbous and covered in fine bristles. The northerner was squatting next to the steed, unawares, lost to everything except the beating of its iron heart. He looked up to see Kyrus running towards him, furry arms pointing furiously. He swung his shaggy head around to see the arachnid horror bearing down.

The warrior's eyes widened as he pitched himself to the side, rolling on the hard ground just off the courtyard. The glistening spike at the end of the scorpion's tail buried itself in the steed's leather seat. Mortu came to a crouch, muscles coiled like iron springs. Ruefully he regarded the axe in its sheath, strapped on the side of the steed, far out of reach. He drew his dagger as the scorpion wrenched its tail free, trailing cotton from the tear it made.

The creature skittered towards him. The tail lashed again. Mortu dodged the blow and wrapped his thick arm around the end of the tail, grasping the stinger, slick with oozing venom. The scorpion flung the tail from side to side, swinging Mortu off his feet but the warrior would not let go. He winced as the spikes arrayed around the edges of the carapace bit into his flesh. It could not free its tail and lowered Mortu towards its front pincers, two vicious claws that clattered in anticipation of the warrior's flesh.

Mortu grinned in savage anger. "A kiss, then, foul thing!"

He let go of the tail and flung himself toward the many eyed head. The thing shrieked, a keening wail as the barbarian wrapped his thick arm between head and claw. He yelled his war cry and stabbed down into its face again and again. A blow struck his shoulder, the heavy thud of the bulbous end of the tail. The deadly stinger overshot its mark, burying itself into the scorpion's own vile flesh, a mere inch from Mortu's face.

The scorpion bucked in its death throes as ichor flowed from the mess of wounds where once was a many-eyed face. It twisted savagely one last time, sending the barbarian flying, before it curled into a ball and died with a last shrieking hiss.

Mortu lay a moment before standing. Above was a sea of blue broken only by distant, insubstantial clouds that slid across the sky quickly in the high winds. He was alive still.

He stood and walked stiffly to where the scrawling writing lay across the first dome.

"Might this say, 'Beware giant scorpions'?"

Kyrus nodded. "That is one possible interpretation."

"Indeed. I suggest we resume our journey as soon as ready."

"Prudent."

Kyrus scampered to the steed and scaled

the bar where their belongings were lashed. He produced cloth and a small jug of unguent. Mortu sat near the fount of water. Tiny fingers washed the big man's wounds and dabbed them with the pungent stuff.

"One day, my friend, you're going to be a mite too slow and find yourself standing before St. Peter."

"Is he your god of death?"

Kyrus sighed. "I'm not going to dignify that with a response. After these long years on the road you know very well there is no 'god of death' lurking grim within my creed."

Mortu made a wry expression, completely ill fitted to his stern face. "Then who escorts you to the hall of your ancestors?"

"Now you mock me. Never mind, anyway. The Word of God has been presented to you. If you make yourself deaf to its truth then you have only yourself to blame."

"Back home, men talk only of battle and women. In Zantyum they talked of chariot races and politics. All you ever talk about is religion or philosophy."

"Naturally. I am a superior intellect."

The barbarian stood and regarded the monk's handiwork. A line of jagged cuts ran down the inside of his left arm. The redness was already subsiding as his own preternatural physiology worked to close the wounds, aided by Kyrus's ministrations. Mortu was a man bred for war. All his people were. Their former masters had returned to the stars and, like fighting dogs loosed from their kennel, his people were yet guided by the instincts bred into them.

He looked down on his little friend. "Thanks, again."

Kyrus smiled, revealing his small, pointed teeth. "All part of the service."

Mortu threw his long leg over the saddle while Kyrus scurried to his shoulder. The barbarian opened the throttle and the two sped off in a cloud of dust.

The wasteland changed as they rode south. The rocky plateaus amidst endless waste gave way to rolling dunes. The hard-packed road was soon swallowed by the sands. Mortu kept course by following a line of tall poles decorated with tattered lengths of red cloth. The steed made slow progress in the soft sand. The rhythm of the dunes lulled the pair into a near trance when a ridge appeared ahead. Mortu realized with a start that the air held a touch of the sea in its scent. The road returned underneath them as the ground became rocky. Suddenly they were on top of the ridge. Beneath them a long, snaking track was cut into the rock, big enough to accommodate two carts abreast. In the wide basin beneath lay a city, a jumble of square, rectangle, and dome laid out in no discernable pattern or order. Beyond that, a greenish blue haze all the way to the horizon.

Kyrus spoke, "Kwarzim. And the sea beyond."

"Gods, look at that."

Mortu pointed though it was not necessary. Their eyes were drawn to the city's center. There, countless bricks and timbers had been stacked and shaped and mortared and lashed together to form a giant scorpion, tail rising towards the sky. The entire structure was sheathed in gold, gleaming in the desert light. Between its two crude pincers was a wide, circular structure. It was rings upon rings of seats surrounding a flat field, sandy in color.

Mortu smirked, a gesture laden with the fatalism common among those who think little of their fellow man. He spoke, deep voice, heavier than the wind. "An arena."

Kyrus replied, "Perhaps."

He squatted back down on Mortu's shoulder and the barbarian guided the steed down the long track to the city's gates. Soon the press of humanity closed in as the tract converged with others. Braying iljigs, their great bulk sheathed in long, wispy hair, nudged against eight wheeled carts, dusty and rust-streaked contraptions, relics of old technology. Kyrus from his perch thought he saw a black, conical hat, its tall wearer sheathed in robes, standing off to the side. But the sight was immediately lost in the press. He shivered slightly. Such was the garb worn by The Forlorn, those few Illilissy that had stayed behind though their race had left Earth. Some believed they watched and waited in order to tell their brothers and sisters when the time was right to come rule again. Those of a more romantic bent spun theories of broken hearts and the inevitable tragedy of love between mortals and those whose lifespans stretched into eons. All agreed they were formidable, commanding alien magics and possessed of strange devices, and were to be left alone.

The gate loomed ahead. A disinterested guard gave the pair a look up and down and waved them through the stone arch. Mortu inquired about artificers capable of making parts and was pointed toward the artisan's quarter.

"Walk down the Amir's Road, keeping the tail to your right. When you pass the palace bear left."

The northerner thanked the man and headed into the press of the avenue. He looked to the center of the city. The tail of the giant stone scorpion cast a long shadow across the bustling avenue. Colorful signs in the scrawling Azari script advertised goods and services. Mortu grasped the lever that mitigated the steed's massive power and they inched along. They passed a kiosk bedecked in colorful flags. Behind the counter a woman and a child deftly manipulated sticks topped with some substance over a bed of coals. The child darted from behind the banners with a handful of samples. Mortu smiled at the girl and bowed his head as he took one.

Kyrus spoke, pointing at the kiosk, "Careful! If that scrawl is to be believed, that little morsel will set your mouth aflame!"

"It's quite sweet, actually."

Ahead two merchants wearing peaked caps tossed a copper to the girl who returned with a larger portion. They had elongated, smooth faces and alert eyes. They were human in the same way the Mortu was human, a subspecies of man created by the Illilissy.

They were not the only foreigners. Mortu spotted nomads swathed in dusty cloth, only their eyes visible between the sandy folds. There were people from the far east, compact of build and attired in long silks. Kyrus wondered about a group of sailors, fair skinned but with dark hair and wearing the loose shirts and short trousers as did deckhands from far Zantyum. The natives of the city were an attractive lot, olive skinned and bearing strong features. None came anywhere near as tall as Mortu. With a slight sneer he gestured to a group of men milling outside what might have been a house of trading. They wore elaborate robes of fine linen, embellished with vests of damask or complex embroidery. Everywhere was the scorpion motif.

"Their men are soft," he said.

Kyrus shrugged. "It is a city of not insignificant wealth. I am not surprised. These people do not need to fight to the death over of bowl of oats and scrap of venison, as do your blighted group."

Mortu laughed. "While you exaggerate, little friend, I must point out my people once ruled the whole of the earth, after setting the Illilissy to flight."

Kyrus replied, "And then came your squabbling. Thus ended the Age of the Sorcerer Kings."

"The Age of the Machines, the Age of the Il-lilissy, the Age of the Sorcerer Kings. And now, our present. What is the Age that we live now?"

Kyrus shook his head. "You don't name an age whilst it is ongoing, dolt."

"Why not?"

"It just isn't done!"

The braying of a pack beast cut the conversation short. Mortu guided the steed around its scaled bulk, earning a nod of appreciation from a veiled woman who rode atop its thick neck.

Their gaze lingered on the massive scorpion. From their position, a great claw loomed, a golden wall reaching up in gentle curves. From this close Mortu spied slits, narrow openings at irregular points along its gilded length. While the steed idled he tugged on the sleeve of a passing merchant. The man stopped in his tracks and regarded Mortu with frank curiosity.

The northerner asked, "Do people live within the giant scorpion?"

The merchant bore the question with as much dignity as he could muster. In a thick accent he replied. "That is not a 'giant scorpion'. It is a holy representation of Daganha, the god of the desert who watches over the city."

Though the merchant posed no threat to him Mortu was not one to give offence within another's lands.

"I meant no disrespect."

The merchant shook his head. "No, of course not. You are from far away, no doubt." He gestured to the giant sculpture. "To answer your question, within Daganha's great claws await those who have garnered his displeasure. Seven is Daganha's number, and every seven days those within are released upon the sands. There they receive judgment from Daganha's holy children. Now, if you will pardon me I have business." He gestured down the street before leaving. "Go leave a silver at the temple. You will be blessed and you stay here serene and your aims successful. Good day."

He left in a flourish of robe, displaying the quick gait of those of the city, gone in the crowd before Mortu could offer thanks.

Kyrus sniffed and gestured to the massive scorpion. "If only the Word could be spread faster. As Moses was delayed so are my brothers and I. And so this calf appears."

Mortu shrugged. "Gods must be appeased."

Kyrus sighed. "Were the air not so hot and dense and filled with noise I would certainly argue that point."

As the afternoon wore on the streets became even busier. The heat was abating, and more and more residents set about on their errands. Mortu did his best to reign in his irritation as the steed was only able to move at a crawl. Finally the large stone buildings with their ornate fronts gave way to the long warehouses and simple workshops of the artisan's quarter. The crowd trickled to groups of workmen walking the wide street in no hurry. The afternoon sun was just beginning to dip. Mortu made inquiries. Thogon was named as the artificer most skilled in the machines of the Illilissy.

The shop was situated in a warehouse far down the lane. An apprentice met Mortu at the open door and led him inside. His workshop was a mess of wire and hose. A thousand articles of unknown provenance lay jumbled in heaps along the long walls. Sunlight poured in from wide skylights. In one corner the clutter was cleared away, an invisible border where beyond an older woman presided over a domestic scene. A couple of toddlers sat on a woven mat, inexpertly stacking wooden blocks while the woman tended a pot hung above a brazier. A large man sat hunched over a table. Sparks erupted from his wand as he worked on a piece of steel. The apprentice made no move to interrupt so Mortu stood quiet, arms folded. Kyrus sat on his shoulder, shielding his eyes from the dazzling light of the wand.

The work halted and the man removed a mask revealing a long face, deeply lined. He stroked his beard once and regarded his guests.

"Jilly, what have you brought me?"

The apprentice spoke, "An outlander who rides an Illilissy steed. He says the heart ails."

"Indeed? Let's have a look."

He stood and bowed curtly. "I am Thogon," he said.

"Mortu."

Kyrus stood on the shoulder and returned the bow. "Kyrus, at your service, sir."

Thogon's dark eyes brightened. "A talking monkey! Amazing." He looked to Mortu. "How did you accomplish that? How did you teach him to talk?"

Kyrus scoffed. "Ha! Teach me? He himself can barely talk! As a matter of fact, this is the work of dark sorcery."

"Oh." Kyrus was forgotten as the group stepped outside to look at the steed. Thogon gave a long whistle.

"Even under layers of dust and grime she's a beautiful beast." He squatted down to inspect the heart. "Have you had problems with the heart before?" Mortu shook his head no. Thogon continued. "Not surprising. Do you see this particular arrangement? The heart is two chambers, set at angles. This configuration is common from the workshops that outfitted the regiments of northerners. Your people, if I am not mistaken. She might be a thousand years old."

"So I was told."

Kyrus spoke, "You are very knowledgeable."

Thogon shrugged. "Artificers like myself will be unlocking the secrets of the old masters for a long time to come. It helps to know the history, such as it is."

Kyrus nodded. "Much has been lost."

Mortu kicked the beast to life and Thogon listened to its rumbling purr.

The artificer and the barbarian began a discussion regarding the beast's heart. Kyrus stroked his tail as their words gradually became so much noise in his ears, uninterested as he was in the workings of alien technology, discussed by two men of limited intellect. He scampered to the ground and took in the avenue. The pace was languid. Work was being done but in no particular hurry. A short walk from Thogon's shop was a small kiosk. Kyrus watched as hot tea was served by a young woman with a pleasant face, full cheeks betraying a life without hardship. Workmen took the small metal cups to a line of rickety tables where they sat and sipped, talked and argued. Two men sat hunched over their table, brows furrowed in concentration.

Kyrus's tiny black eyes saw that which had engrossed the pair. He felt sudden joy as he darted across the street, narrowly missing the wide rubber wheels of a cart.

Kyrus hopped onto the table. The men reeled back, swearing in the tongue of the city. The pair had been playing chess.

"What new vermin is this? Shooo! Scorpion take you!"

Kyrus raised his arms for mercy. He replied in their tongue, halting and accent odd, but intelligible.

"A thousand pardons, good sirs! I wish only

to take in your game. I love chess! For years, it was the only diversion permitted to me during my long studies in the…"

He sought the right word, realizing 'monastery', in Imperial, had no direct correspondence in Kwarzimi.

"He talks!"

"Thank Daganha that you also hear it. I thought I was going mad." The man turned to address Kyrus. "Are you a creature from the wastes?"

"He is an imp from Hell."

Other men had abandoned their tea and conversation to gather around the table. Theories were essayed in rapid succession.

"He is a monkey from the far jungles of Bopo. I saw it in a book once. It made no mention of the ability to speak, although perhaps it did, and I simply forgot."

"He is young specimen of an Apeman from Sheesied."

"He's no monkey or Apeman, you simpletons. He is a pet, bred to amuse the departed Masters. They must have left him behind so long ago."

"That would make him nigh on a thousand years old, dimwit."

"The White Lords were capable of such, and more!"

Kyrus raised his arms and shouted above the din.

"Gentlemen! Gentlemen, please!" The display brought quiet. "Now, if you must know,

I was once a man, such as yourselves, though very educated. I incurred the anger of a great sorcerer and was thus imprisoned in this body, which is in fact that of a common monkey."

The man who had guessed monkey nodded in deep satisfaction.

Kyrus continued, "My friend and I are traveling east to seek a remedy for the curse. Surely it is all God's will, as during the journey I may also bring God's word to places where the old masters have taken it from man's imperfect memory."

The men looked at each other, eyes wide in alarm. The first one that had spoken, one of the chess players, leaned toward Kyrus.

"We understand outside the city there are many gods, many creeds, but in the city one must only speak of Daganha."

Another man spoke, "My friend does you a great favor by telling you this. The law is enforced most assiduously. If any citizen hears anything against Daganha he need only write the name of the offender on a slip of paper and place it the black boxes that sit outside every shrine. The next day priests will come and take the person to sit in The Claws and await judgment."

Kyrus spoke, "The system would seem vulnerable to abuse."

"Oh, indeed. Periodically a jealous lover or business rival may be tempted to slip in a name or two. Their guilt is invariably found out and punishment is meted. On top of all that"—here the man paused, looking around a moment then bending close—"there are spies everywhere. People joke that though the tail can be seen from everywhere in the city, the scorpion's reach goes farther.

Kyrus thought to ask about the punishment but lost courage. He shuddered a moment and then remembered himself. "I shall have to be circumspect. It will be taxing, as my conscious demands that I bring the good news to whomever may hear."

Sight of the chess board brought him back to the present.

"Well, would any of my new friends care to join me in a game?"

The ring glittered in the rays of streaking sunlight that poured in from the skylight. It was nearly the size of Mortu's wrist. A thin crack snaked its way along nearly the whole length of it. He held it in his grimy hands, stained black from the steed's blood. Thogon looked on in wonder. On the floor before them the parts of the steed's heart were laid out on a cloth. The artificer had disassembled the heart with Mortu's help.

"Bright iron."

Mortu looked at the artificer in puzzlement.

"That is what we call this metal here. It is from the Illilissy. The secret of its crafting returned with them to the stars. The crack causes a loss in pressure in the heart's innermost chambers. The beat grows irregular. It may take you another thousand leagues or shatter tomorrow and wreck the heart completely.

The barbarian knew the word for bright iron in the old masters' tongue. A bastard form of the speech was the language of his people. But matters of language were not on his mind.

"Do you have a replacement for this ring?"

Thogon laughed. "Bright iron is a hundred times more precious than gold. Had I a store of it I would live in a palace in the shade of the Tail, and not here, near the docks."

The northerner shook his head. "I did not anticipate this, though I should have. In my home great stocks of parts and other ephemera still remain. Naturally it is not so in the rest of the world." He held the ring up. "Is there an alternative? Could you fashion a ring of plain steel?"

Thogon stepped to a metal box. His hands gestured to the levers and switches that sprung from its ancient surface. "I can machine nearly anything. But the pressures in the steed's heart will make short work of mundane steel."

Mortu's fist clenched and his brow furrowed.

Thogon continued. "There is one nearby who may have what you need."

The barbarian looked up.

"His name is Oram. He is perhaps the wealthiest man in the city. Only the high priests wield more influence than Oram. He is a great collector and a scholar of sorts. People say he owns one of everything."

"Where can I find this man?"

Thogon stepped onto the street with the barbarian in tow. He pointed to an area opposite the gleaming tail.

"Do you see that quarter? See the artful towers? There the wealthy call home. Each mansion seeks to outdo the other. Oram lives in a palace bedecked with blue tile."

"To the matter of payment, I have some coin from Zantyum. It seems rather paltry for a man of your skill."

Thogon waved his hand. "I'm sure we can come to an agreement."

Mortu thanked the artificer and made to leave. Thogon urged caution.

"If accosted by a priest, beg forgiveness and plead the innocence of an outlander. And be careful. People say Oram is a greedy man, and without scruples. They say he spoils his grandchildren, so perhaps somewhere is good in his heart." The artificer lowered his voice to a whisper and continued, "But his behavior dishonors Daganha though the priests give him a wide berth. Doubtless he pays for their favor."

Mortu shrugged. "Such an arrangement seems common in cities. Whenever men replace natural law they soon become a servant to wealth." He met the artificer's eyes and gave thanks. Thogon looked on in puzzlement. He called into the street as the barbarian left.

"What is 'natural law'"

Mortu looked over his shoulder as his hand patted the axe hung at his waist.

Thogon shook his head as he stepped to the area where his grandchildren played. He took up his granddaughter in his heavy arms as she squealed and laughed. The young man was honest and likeable despite his brusque northerner's ways. Thogon wondered whether Mortu would survive the city.

Along with the difficulty of finding the ring, Mortu found himself burdened with the problem of finding a small monkey somewhere in a city of a hundred thousand souls. How long had he been working with Thogon? Perhaps a few hours, going by the sun. From experience Mortu knew a few hours was more than enough time for the monk to get himself into serious trouble. The barbarian strolled the avenue hoping to catch a glimpse of his small friend. Traffic in the artisan's quarter had picked up as people were out and about, on their way to market for their evening's supper. Mortu stood head and shoulders above most in the crowd which did him no good in the search for one only as high as his knee. His own stomach growled as the afternoon wore on. Soon he found himself outside the artisan's quarter and decided to double back. If Kyrus was not in trouble then doubtless the arrogant monk would make his own way back to Thogon's shop.

The smell of grilled meat carried him past the shop to a nearby kiosk. A crowd had gathered around the tables. Mortu stepped to kiosk but the girl spoke no Imperial, nor did Mortu possess any local coin. Irritated, the barbarian tugged at the sleeve of a merchant. The man seemed eager to press forward through the crowd and indulge himself in whatever spectacle so entertained the gaggle.

"What is this?"

The man gave him a look of incomprehension for the briefest of moments before his mind understood the foreign tongue.

He replied back in a thick accent, "There is a monkey at the tables who plays chess! Whoever heard of such a thing!"

Mortu shook his head. "I have."

"A wonder!"

"Trust me. It gets old."

The barbarian pushed his way through the press. At the center Kyrus hopped among three tables. Each had a board and opponent. Hop, move, hop, move, and soon a "checkmate!" The crowd applauded each victory, laughing at his quick banter as he pondered the next move or consoled the vanquished. Mortu watched the spectacle, arms folded.

Kyrus looked up. "Ah, my young friend. Is your beloved machine back in good health?"

"Not quite. We must see a wealthy man and buy, beg, or barter for a part. His name is Oram and he lives somewhere on the other side of the tail."

Kyrus took in the sky. A band of warm ochre hugged the horizon over the far sea. A darkening violet rose over the band. Night was perhaps an hour away.

"I wonder if he will mind guests at this hour."

Mortu shrugged. The crowd egged him on and Kyrus gave his full attention back to the boards and their crudely carved pieces. Shortly, all three games were brought to a decisive conclusion. Kyrus stood and bowed to the crowd, begging an end to the entertainment. He hopped to Mortu's shoulder as the crowd began to disperse. Occasionally someone pressed a coin into the barbarian's hand. His cheeks burned but the slight was not enough to dissuade him from handing the coins over to the girl behind the counter.

Presently the pair strolled the avenue. Mortu ate grilled meat off a long skewer while Kyrus worked on a plum-like fruit, perhaps twice as big as his head. The business of the day was slowly giving way to the diversions of the night. Families were settled down to supper, windows open to the cool breeze in their apartments, stacked three or four high. The buildings were sturdy, tan brick embellished with colored tile, in harmony with the desert to the north and a compliment to the blue-green sea to the south. Young men and women gathered in the numerous public spaces, water founts, and small gardens, where they socialized, enacting the delicate rituals that would move them inexorably to their own families and suppers and apartments.

Ahead the traffic had parted for a procession. At their head was a youth, cowl down to reveal a shaved head, censer swinging in the evening air. Black-robed men walked in step with each other. In the center eight burly specimens bore a palanquin. Following behind the censer-bearing youth was a curious sight. A scorpion, as big as a warhound, walked its strange, eight legged gait. To either side were young men in cowls like the youth that bore the incense. They carried rods of bamboo upon which were affixed balls of red leather, ends slick with some sort of oil. The young men held the balls hovering near the head of the scorpion and so seemed to guide it. The terrible creature was placid, strolling the lane with no more fuss than a pony or mule. Mortu recoiled at the sight of it, ochre carapace bristling with black hairs.

Behind it eight men walked with heads held high. Kohl rimmed eyes scanned all before them with an air of studied superiority. Heavy blades capped by jeweled hilts hung from thick belts trimmed in gold. Upon their chest, embroidered in rich gold, was the scorpion.

Mortu spoke, "The priests."

"A rather menacing lot."

A chime sounded and the procession halted. From the palanquin emerged a large man in black robes hemmed in gold, armed as the others. He locked eyes with Mortu. There was a sudden frisson in the air as happens when armed and warlike men meet as strangers. He came to stand before Mortu as the procession stood still and unmoving, like the legionaries of Zantyum.

The robes could not hide his powerful physique. He stood there a moment then addressed Mortu.

"Outlander."

His Imperial had no trace of accent. Mortu studied the face. Underneath a strong brow eyes colored the blue of glacier stared back at the barbarian. The man was deeply tanned but the bones underneath betrayed him.

The priest was of the Men of the North. Mortu strangled his shock before it showed on his face.

Mortu spoke, "We are far from home. I did not ever expect to see one of my kind here."

The priest laughed low as he shook his head.

"Nor did I. It has been many years since I laid eyes on one of my own kind. Seeing a countryman recalls how troublesome our people can be. Always fighting and upsetting things."

Mortu smiled. "Indeed, the same thought occurred to me."

Their conversation was interrupted by Kyrus's sputtering.

"Wow! What are the odds?"

The priest looked with annoyance at the interruption. "Quiet your imp."

Kyrus spoke, "Imp! It must be unbearable in the North, everyone so rude and curt."

The priest ignored him. "What brings you to Kwarzim?"

"My iron steed ails."

"That explains why you are here in my city. But why did you leave home?"

"I slew my brother. Rather than watch the clan descend into feud, I left."

The priest nodded. "I knew you had the look of an outlaw. I see it myself in every reflection."

Mortu spoke, "And why did you leave?"

The priest stepped to the scorpion's side. He stroked the gnarled carapace of its head. Mortu felt his skin crawl as he heard the thing softly chitter in response.

He spoke. "I found our home inadequate to my ambition." He switched to the tongue native to the land of their birth and continued. "When fate took me here I saw much opportunity. The priests were weak. They had never seen one like us, one born to rule. I showed them strength, showed them the potential in their cult. Now we are feared throughout the city. I have wealth and women aplenty. The high priest grows more feeble everyday." He stood and stared deep into Mortu's eyes. He seemed to look for something. Mortu showed no emotion.

The priest had Mortu's curious gift, to make a smile seem like a threat. He smiled and spoke, "When your steed is fixed I suggest you depart."

From his perch on the barbarian's shoulder Kyrus could feel the big man's muscles tense.

"I'll leave when it suits me."

"Indeed, you will. Fair travels, countryman." He stepped to the palanquin.

Mortu called after him. "Your name?"

"Here I am Dhuden. Back home I was Svar-jere."

"I am Mortu."

"I know."

He stepped inside and another chime sounded. The group departed.

Mortu stood staring after them.

Kyrus spoke. "What was his name? I always found your language so difficult."

"Svarjere. It means 'black hearted' in the old tongue."

"Indeed! For a moment, I thought you two would come to blows. It's a wonder that any of your people live to continue the race. There is a no more fractious lot. Why did he stare at you so?"

Mortu watched the group disappear around a corner.

He spoke, "He thought I might be impressed and wish to join him."

The pair continued on. Above them the tail loomed as the residences became more splendid. Where the apartments boasted a picturesque similarity, the palaces sought each to carve out its own niche, wildly different in style and execution. Here the streets were lined with tall poles decorated like palms. At the end of the street a few had begun to glow. Kyrus marveled as their workings were revealed.

He watched as a young man shimmied up a nearby pole with practiced ease. He locked his

skinny legs around its width and reached behind his back where a heavy skin was slung.
He pulled a cap free with his mouth and tipped
the skin, filling a reservoir hidden in the ornate
top. There was a buzzing sound as an insect,
perhaps half the size of a man's fist, came to
rest at the top. Its head disappeared over the
rim and moments later its abdomen began to
glow. It was joined by another, then another,
and soon the cup was ringed by insects. He
slid down and made for the next pole. Soon
the wide avenue was bathed in a yellow glow.

Ahead Mortu spied a palace of blue tile, all
the way at the end of the street. A small crowd
milled around before its walled grounds. Mortu and Kyrus approached a gilded gate where
a stiff backed, powerful bureaucrat stood,
flanked by guards in resplendent gold scale.
The feathers on their tall helms stirred slightly
in the gentle breeze from the bay. The man in
charge, the bureaucrat, was tall and thin, red
robes trimmed in gold.

Kyrus spoke near Mortu's ear. "This line of
people must be waiting to see Oram. He must
be a powerful patron."

Mortu grunted. "We have no time for this."
He stepped before the red robed man and
made to speak. The guards stepped forward.
Crisp movements brought their spears to the
fore, crossed in front of Mortu's path. The barbarian growled.

Kyrus hopped to the ground and raised his
arms. His high voice cut through the evening

air. "Gentlemen! I beg your forbearance! My friend and I are unschooled in the ways of your fair city. We wish only a word with the great Oram."

The red robed man peered down at Kyrus. "Are you a mutant from the waste or the work of a sorcerer?"

"The latter."

"Interesting. I imagine he had quite a sense of humor."

"I can't say I was particularly amused."

The man laughed a moment then made a languid gesture toward the milling crowd. "You must wait with everyone else lest this small mob become enraged."

The audience was over. A small man stepped past Mortu to stand before the red-robed man. He spread his arms wide in a piteous gesture and began to spin a tale of sudden poverty.

The muscles in Mortu's jaw twitched as the pair made their way to the back.

"How long will this take?"

Kyrus exhaled long as he pondered the crowd. "Impossible to know. Each supplicant will likely take a different amount of time. The hour grows late. I have a feeling those of us at the end of the line have scant hope of speaking with Oram's flunky this evening."

Mortu became pensive. "We could come back tomorrow. But a strange foreboding grows in me. A dark heart beats behind the pleasant façade of this city."

Kyrus made a flippant gesture. "You say

that about everywhere."

"And often as not I am right. We must get the part as soon as able and leave, as much as it pains me that I seem to bend to Svarjere's will."

"I shall miss the chess."

The line moved slowly. Along with inactivity Mortu had to suffer constant stares, stolen over the shoulder, as the other supplicants wondered at the strange pair. His mind wandered.

The barbarian thought of his steed, sitting idle. He remembered the day it was given to him. He stood before Gouroth, the favorite of his brother's hearth guard. The old warrior smiled as Mortu's hands gripped the beast's metal horns. The shamans' voices droned on as they did the rituals necessary to join warrior and steed so that the beast would respond to Mortu's touch. He remembered smiling despite the solemnity of the conversation. He remembered his brother smiling too, bedecked in a coat of bright iron. Mortu lowered his head. The memories continued.

In his mind's eye he watched. Through falling leaves he saw the hot spring where he came upon his brother's favorite wife, bathing. Steam rose from her shoulders in the autumn chill.

Kyrus tugged at his ear. The monk's voice came sudden and sharp into his ear.

"Step aside!"

Mortu snapped out of his reverie. Sheepishly he stepped aside as a cart wheeled past. It was tall and narrow, colors garish even in the soft light of the avenue's strange lamps. Ahead the guards had made a path through the crowd as the hulking drays snorted through their scaly noses.

The gilded gates stood open.

Kyrus harangued his tall friend. "Are you ill? The driver shouted and shouted."

Mortu shook his head. "My mind wandered back all the way my home."

The monk's voice softened. "Oh. I'm sorry, young man."

The barbarian shrugged.

"Well, young man, what I am about to say, I have said many times before. I know it is hard but you should look to the future. The past cannot be changed. And as the good Lord teaches us, grace is possible for all. Your sins were paid for long before you were even born."

"I have made no 'sin'. My brother's blood was spilled in a lawful duel."

"Yes, as you have explained before. But if things were so simple then why…"

A shrill voice interrupted the monk.

"What are you?"

The pair turned. From an open panel on the cart a small face peered at Kyrus. The monk stared dumbly.

"Mommy, what is he?"

A woman, barely visible in the dim light, crowded next to the child, attempting to pull her away from the window.

"It is nothing to do with us, Pinxie. Now, get back in your seat. We are almost home."

"But he's so funny!" The face was beaming. She had the wide eyes and warm olive skin of the city people.

"Pinxie! Sit back, at once!"

Kyrus felt a chill. Her big eyes glistened with want.

"Get him for me!" There was a scuffle as the girl fought the shadowy matrons who sought to restrain her. "I want to give him a piece of my candy!"

"Do so and then get back in your seat, dear girl."

Half leaning out of the window the girl reached towards Kyrus, a jelly suffused with candied rind pinched between her squat fingers.

Mortu laughed, "Come on, old man, do not be rude! Accept your gift."

Kyrus took the candy.

"Eat it! Eat it!"

Mortu smiled, "The little girl is greatly amused by you, old man. Entertainer of children! Another possible career for you! Such joy you could bring!"

"I speak a dozen languages! I have studied libraries of texts from before the arrival of the Illilissy! Me and mine are on a holy quest to bring this lost world back into God's warm grace! I am no clown to caper for the delight of children!"

With solemn expression Kyrus ate the candy.

"He ate it! I want him! I want him!"

Mortu laughed as the cart moved again, voices inside becoming more strident as the child protested.

Kyrus cursed as his little fingers fidgeted in his mouth. "Damned bit of rind stuck in my teeth."

The ornate gates slammed shut behind the cart.

The red robed man spoke over his shoulder to another aide and turned back to address the crowd. His voice was heavy with authority as he spoke. "There will be no more audiences tonight. Daganha willing, you may come again tomorrow when the sun dips beneath the tail."

The barbarian's mirth evaporated.

Kyrus sighed. "We best find somewhere to bed down."

He made inquiries of the disappointed supplicants. A man named Yarma invited them to follow him. He was bald and of lanky build. A pall hung around him. Mortu thought him one of those poor souls perpetually outside of the favor of any gods. Bad luck.

In a tired voice he explained. "Those of us that find ourselves temporarily of limited means may find shelter in the temple by the docks. I myself must lodge there this evening due to the acrimonious environment that presides at my once-happy home."

Kyrus debated with himself whether or not to ask the source of the trouble and likely trigger an unburdening from the man.

Yarma spared him the decision. He continued in a reedy voice, speaking in Imperial for the benefit of Mortu.

The barbarian had been correct in his first impression. The man spun a tale of failed business and an enraged spouse. He and his confreres pooled their resources to explore the surrounding desert for hidden sources of fresh water.

"Thousands of years ago this area was green. The Old Masters worked their sorcery and now it is desert. But is it not likely that the water was merely hidden? It is underground, as it was when Daganha laid the egg from which the earth hatched."

Kyrus nodded approval. "I imagine you are right. At what point did the scheme go awry?"

Yarma scanned the street. In a markedly softer voice he continued. "The priests. My idea was deemed an affront to the will of Daganha. Our money was made a gift to the temple to atone for our hubris. Every penny I had. Galina was irate. I can't say I blame her." Yarma shrugged, a gesture particularly suited to his narrow shoulders. He continued. "Oh, well. She'll cool down and I'll get back on my feet. Always do." His warm grin showed two missing teeth.

Kyrus nodded and spoke, " 'Be joyful in hope, patient in affliction, faithful in prayer.'"

Yarma's ambling gait led them back to the district of shops and warehouses. Off a side street was a long, one story building in bad repair. The sign above the door showed another scorpion. Its thick abdomen was covered with tiny young.

An older woman in shabby priest's robes took a coin from Mortu and the three spent the night on palettes on the hard floor. A single oil lamp in the center of the room illuminated a scene of rising and falling backs, rough breath in the chill air of the desert night. Kyrus and Yarma slept soon as Mortu sat brooding, regarding the night through a window of cheap glass.

The city's destitute woke at dawn to seek work. Yarma bid the pair farewell as he set off to regain his wealth and the love of his wife.

Mortu and Kyrus strode through the morning traffic. The northerner paid two coppers to a smoky stall and made a breakfast of roasted lizard. Kyrus demurred. Mortu sat on a low wall. The sandy bricks curved artfully around a bed of dirt from which sprouted flowering shrubs. The wide plaza touched four of the city's districts and all classes and professions mingled in the press, coming and going, cells moving through the heart of the city with the rhythm of the day.

Mortu twitched with boredom as the pair lounged, killing time until the sun dipped just below the tail which loomed above. Above the crowd Mortu's eye caught long feathers swaying. The crowd shuffled aside and there stood the man in red robes, Oram's functionary, flanked by two of the plumed guards. The man's eyes met Mortu and the northerner watched relief spread across pinched features. He came to stand before the two. Kyrus dozed, chin in hand, leaning on Mortu's thigh like a drunk at the bar.

Mortu did not stand but sat up, feet planted and arms loose at his sides. The red robed man came before him. He bowed.

"I am Huj, aide to Oram the Wise, Blessed of Daganha."

Mortu nodded and gave his name. With his finger he gave the monk a gentle flick.

"And this is Kyrus."

"Wha? How long was I out? Who is this?"

"His name is Huj."

Kyrus squinted. "You are the gentleman we attempted to speak with last night."

"Indeed. Word reached my master about the pair of outlanders wishing to see him. My master feels there has been a breach of hospitality. Travelers such as yourself deserve a better reception."

Kyrus stood and spoke, "I agree!"

Mortu said nothing, regarding Huj with his cold eyes.

The red robed man continued. "Might I ask, out of curiosity, what brings you to the city?"

"My friend's iron steed grows ill and we seek to repair it. Apparently it needs a part of blight iron, which your master is said to possess, or have the ability to procure."

"Bright iron," corrected Mortu.

Kyrus shrugged as Huj replied, "Ah! Indeed you are correct. My master's stocks of rare materials is the envy of the entire world."

Mortu spoke, "I wonder what your master will ask for this boon."

Kyrus continued the thought, "I hope nothing too dear. My friend and I are traveling with regrettably limited means."

"And where are you going?"

"We seek a remedy for a sorcerous affliction. As I mentioned last night, some years ago my soul was imprisoned in this body you see before you."

Huj nodded thoughtfully. "Far to the east there might be men wise enough to aid you."

"My thoughts exactly."

Huj licked his lips and spoke, "Well, the hour is young. Please accept my master's hospitality while we await the hour when he receives guests."

"We will indeed!"

Huj gestured to the plaza. Kyrus scrambled up to sit at his usual perch. The barbarian shot him a wary glance but the monk was oblivious.

Kyrus spoke, "What do you have in this city in the way of fresh fruit? I'm a bit peckish."

Huj smiled and set off, Mortu and Kyrus in tow. The barbarian glanced back to see the guards following. They kept a polite distance though the northerner noted the tension in their arms.

The man led them across the plaza and along a wide avenue lined with tall palms. The shops here had traded their tent roofs for tiles of red clay. Many facades boasted wide glass windows. The cames, the lead bars holding the glass, were bent in fanciful curves, perhaps waves from the near bay or wind-swept dunes,

Mortu could not decide.

Huj turned down an alley and the group found themselves in an alehouse, largely empty. Mortu grunted approval as he seated himself on a bench. A veiled woman brought the group mugs of beer. Huj gave thanks and made Kyrus's needs known.

The barbarian threw the mug back and drank deep. The stuff was cool and light, an antidote for the harsh sun and close air of the city. He motioned for another as Huj regarded him. His small, gray eyes looked from under raised eyebrows.

Kyrus chuckled, "Do not mind my friend. He rarely drinks to excess. For a fact, his peculiar lineage grants him great stamina."

Huj replied, "Is that so? So it is true what they say about the Men of the North?"

Kyrus wiped water from his chin and began to speak. He saw his friend's eyes go dark, glaring at him from under his strong brow.

A tray of fruit and bread was placed before Kyrus. He rubbed his hands in anticipation and set to work, first selecting a slice of orange shot through with red veins. Mortu tore at a loaf of hearty bread.

Kyrus, mouth full, replied to Huj, "Very possibly. But, tell us about your master."

"Oh, Oram. He is a powerful man. I am lucky to be in his service," He paused, noticing Mortu's empty mug. "Allow me."

The ceiling was open. Through slats of dark timber sheathed in crawling ivy came the yellow light particular to this area, harsh like the desert but tinged with moisture from the bay. Huj's thin frame strode through the dappled light towards the bar. The two guards sat at the end of the bench, watching Mortu as they gingerly sipped their beer.

Huj placed Mortu's mug before him with a flourish.

"Drink up, outlander. It is bought with Oram's coin."

Mortu nodded and took up the mug.

His deep voice seemed over loud in the intimate quiet of the alehouse.

"What will your master want for the bright iron?"

Huj shrugged. "Though I imagine he has already made up his mind," said Mortu.

His keen eyes studied the barbarian as he quaffed his beer. Mortu slammed the mug down and wiped his mouth with tanned forearm.

Huj's eyebrows arched again. He looked to the guards who then looked to each other.

The thin man spoke, "Well, another perhaps?"

Mortu nodded. Huj stepped again to the bar and returned. He pushed the heavy mug towards Mortu. The northerner took up the mug and drained it. Huj and the guards watched him.

Kyrus remarked upon the fruit. "Now, this here is delicious. Sweet and tart, but not too much. It fills the belly and wets the throat equally well. At my home in Zantyum there is something similar but the fruit tends to be larger and thus the flavor less, bold, less concentrated perhaps."

Huj kept his eyes on Mortu even as he replied to Kyrus. "You are quite the connoisseur."

Kyrus shrugged, "You would be too, were you to walk the earth with a monkey's palette. Oddly, I do not miss the foods I used to enjoy. Thinking of them…"

Mortu slammed his fists down upon the table, sending mugs and trays aloft.

"Poison! I feel my heart slow. You treacherous fop!"

Huj fell from the bench in his haste to flee Mortu's advance, crawling backwards on the floor. Behind the big barbarian the guards stood, drawing weapons.

Despite his evident fear, the thin man laughed.

"I was wondering if it would ever take effect. You've had enough to kill two men. I just wanted you to sleep, you wretched son of the invader!"

Mortu drew his axe. But his step faltered and he collapsed to sit on the bench. The guards watched warily, frozen in positions of readiness.

The barbarian fell to the floor. Kyrus hopped down to stand beside him. Mortu's face was twisted with the vain effort to force his muscles to move against the grip of the poison. The big man growled until finally his eyes closed and his body went limp with a final sigh.

Huj stood and brushed his robes. Kyrus stared up at him and then at the fruit still in his hand.

The thin man smiled, "No poison for you. Just a sack."

He motioned to the guards and they took up the monkey, stuffing him roughly into a burlap sack. Kyrus fought, kicking and scratching at the cloth. He cried out at the pain as the sack was bashed against the table. He heard Huj's voice.

"That was only a tap. Make trouble and these men will smash you against the stones of the street until you are a pulp."

Kyrus let his body sink into the bottom of the sack. He sighed and rubbed his bruises as he was carried out to the avenue.

Under his breath he spoke, "The Lord shall fight for you, and ye shall keep your peace…"

There was darkness, and the feeling that a blade or spike lay lodged in his skull. The light was blinding when he opened his eyes and sent waves of shock that seemed to coil around his spine and settle in his gut. The feeling ebbed away and his eyes adjusted. He found himself in dim coolness. There was stone under him, dust and dirt. The light which had blinded him streaked in from window high on the stone wall. Elsewhere was dim. As his eyes adjusted he realized he was not alone. Leaning against the walls and sprawled or seated on the floor were dozens of men and women. Mortu did not need more light to read the despair on their faces or the dejection plain in the bodies, slack and still. He stood, feeling the poison wane, finally overcome by his inhuman constitution, a gift to his people from their long-ago masters.

"Where am I?"

After a moment a voice answered, Imperial nearly unintelligible from its thick accent.

"You are in the Scorpion's Claw."

Mortu stared at the man who spoke. He was doughy with middle age and dressed in what was once a fine set of robes.

The man continued, "The Claw." He pointed to the gloom of the far end, where the walls gently tapered to meet at a set of odd doors. "In two days time all of us here, will depart through those doors to be judged by Daganha."

"Why am I here?" Mortu suppressed an animal panic, the revulsion of confinement, as he studied his surroundings.

"Do you not know? You have offended the priests, or perhaps one of their friends."

A man leaning against the opposite wall hissed at the speaker. "Watch what you say, Gummot. We are not here because of the priests but because of Daganha's divine will."

"Oh, Julk, your naiveté is positively offensive in our current surroundings. I know my own heart is pure, yet here I am."

Mortu spoke to the one known as Gummot, "What is it you are saying?"

The middle aged man switched back to imperial. "A theological debate, nothing more."

Mortu snorted, "It's a shame my friend is not here." He shook his head, wondering where might the monk be. He looked to the ray of light spilling in from the bars.

"Gods, protect my friend and I will spill oceans of blood in your names."

The sound of quiet sobbing reached the barbarian's ears. The woman sat in the far corner. Fine silks lay in tatters around her. From under her veil embellished in gold she peered at the northerner.

He spoke, "And why are you here?"

Gummot answered for her, "She was a priest's favorite whore and they had a row."

With a shriek she stood and flung herself across the room. Her blows were ineffective, though no less impressive for their fury, as she struck at Gummot.

"I am no whore! I was lover to Azull, Master of Incense, Master of the Rite of Preparation!"

The merchant changed his tone as he fended off the blows.

"Apologies, woman! Calm yourself!" She stepped away, anger and sadness competing across her fine features.

Gummot smoothed out his robes. "My own anger has made me unkind. Alas! We are cursed."

Mortu asked, "Might you be judged innocent?"

The question was met with scattered snickering from the crowd.

"Outlander, Daganha is not known for his mercy."

The one called Julk spoke. "If we were completely innocent, we would not be here."

"Speak for yourself!" Others chimed in and the condemned fell to arguing amongst themselves.

"Silence!" Mortu's voice reverberated in the dim chamber.

In the sudden quiet he spoke again, "Is there no way out?"

Gummot replied, "No, my new friend. We all must meet our fate."

Mortu snarled as he stared at the ray of light. "This is not my fate."

Julk spoke in a forlorn voice, "In two days we will undergo the Rite of Preparation and be brought before Daganha's children. They will search our hearts and know what evil lurks therein. They know. They see your deepest secrets and judge without mercy."

The woman snorted and made a gesture, dismissing the words with callous contempt.

Julk became animated, "It is true!"

She turned on him, eyes afire, and spoke, "You fool! I shared a bed with the Master of Preparation! He was as talkative as he was arrogant! The secrets of this cursed temple are mine! And knowing what I know, you are the greatest fool that ever was!"

Her chest heaved from the volume and venom of her words. Mortu stepped before her.

"What is your name?"

She stood straight and faced him, "Ulkya. Who are you?" Her imperial was barely accented. She was educated, a daughter of privilege.

"I am Mortu. Tell me what you know of this place."

The sack was upended and Kyrus spilled out into light and air. There was a moment of disorientation as his fall was arrested by silk cushions.

He blinked in the sudden light and tried to take in his surroundings. There was Huj in front of him flanked by the guards. On the left was another figure, a man of great bulk. The warm light shone on his bald pate. The thick features of his heavy face sat on broad shoulders without the need for a neck. He wore orange pantaloons below a vest of purple damask. A strange softness afflicted his eyes and mouth. Eunuch, thought Kyrus. The giant stood with arms folded, regarding Kyrus without emotion.

Huj spoke, reedy voice heavy with authority. "Now, sir. Let me describe to you your new life."

"New life! Pah! Release me, at once! I have powerful friends back home! And I will not even speak of my traveling companion! The northerner works in violence like some artists work in oils or marble! You will pay for this outrage!"

"Your friend will be dead in two days. And no one in far Zantyum will ever learn of your fate."

Kyrus gulped with worry for Mortu.

Huj continued, "So, please, for your own

sake cease this pointless bluffing. Your life begins today. You have your work, as I have mine, and Trunk has his," The thin man motioned to the hulking eunuch. Do your work, and you will be rewarded with comfort, safety, and a measure of luxury far greater than the average person will experience. On balance, you should be thankful."

Kyrus stood with arms folded.

"My master loves one thing above all. His family. His grandchildren are a particular delight to him. You will serve his will by entertaining his granddaughter."

"I'm sorry, what?"

"Look around."

The monk did as ordered. The room was spacious, the size of a banquet hall. At intervals delicate columns carved to look like palms spread their artful leaves up into the tall ceiling, decorated with geometric patterns. The floor was laid with dozens of rugs and carpets and fine pelts of soft fur. Great chests lined the walls, trimmed with gold. A few stood open, spilling their contents onto the floor.

Toys. Animals and babies, knights, damsels, dragons, carved in wood or made from cloth with great artistry.

A pair of servants entered through the gold doors. They were bald like Trunk but of slight build. They carried another chest between them.

They set their burden down before Huj and one bent to open it for his inspection. Inside were clothes of all description, robes trimmed in gold, fit for a king, merchant's robes, sea-faring garb, a squire's blouse and coullottes, a costume a prince might wear to go hunting, garments for all occasions.

The servant spoke, "These are all the doll clothes to be had in the entire market. The shops are at work making more, should these not fit."

Huj lifted a small silk shirt from the chest and held it up, turning to appraise Kyrus.

"I think these should be fine. Don't you think so, Kyrus?"

The monk regarded all with eyes wide with horror.

The thin man kneeled to speak to him. His face hovered near. "Oram dotes on his grandchild. Her happiness is of the utmost importance. Do you understand me?"

Kyrus could only manage a small nod.

"Good. You will be her companion. I can't say I envy your position, but this is what fate has wrought and you have no choice but to obey and make the best of it. You will obey her every whim. You will make her laugh, you will delight her, and Oram will be pleased. If you fail in this, if you offend her, if you displease her, Trunk will tear you apart, slow as he pleases. Do you understand? I shan't explain this all again. There will be no warnings. Do what you must or die a painful death."

Huj stood. "Now, with that unpleasantness out of the way, let us talk of something joyous. Today is Oram's granddaughter's birthday. A great celebration is underway even as we speak." Another servant entered bearing a colorful box. Huj smiled.

"Perfect! Our timing is fair. Young Pinxie is unwrapping presents as we speak. Now, why don't we dress you as a prince before you get in the box which will be presented to her. What a grand surprise you will be! No clockwork bear or pet from faraway lands could rival you!"

Kyrus stood stock still.

The thin man cocked his head and asked, "Are you quite alright?"

Kyrus shook his head. "I am wrestling with the notion that I have passed away and awoken in perdition."

"I assure you that you haven't." Huj bent low, a pair of sequined trousers held before him. He saw Kyrus's hesitation. The man arched a single eyebrow and turned slightly towards Trunk.

With a long sigh, Kyrus stepped into the trousers.

"That's a pity."

Well into the night they spoke, huddled close. The barbarian hungered for details of their monstrous prison, a claw of the towering scorpion that served as the center of the city's religious life. She spun the tale of her life, a concubine to a powerful priest. Ulkya was possessed of the kind of beauty that set mens' hearts to beating. Her large, expressive eyes were situated under a delicately arched brow. An impish nose and full lips completed the picture. Dark curls tumbled down from the tatters of her diaphanous veil as the tale unraveled. The priest, a man named Azull, was sweet at first. He showered gifts upon the young woman until she allowed herself to become bent to his will. They made an arrangement. When his duties permitted he stole away to an apartment he procured for her, a luxurious spot with views of the bay. The housing along the beach formed something like an artists' quarter and was favored by the priests for keeping their concubines. They were forbidden to marry but no High Priest saw fit to completely deny themselves earthly pleasure. Ulkya's former lover had made good use of her sympathetic ear. During quiet nights, Azull would lay on their bed as the cool wind from the bay set the window silks gently billowing. He would vent, bitterly, describing a litany of perceived injustices in the priesthood. Though Master of Preparation was a high position, Azull's ambition was far from sated. He resented Dhuden most of all, the outlander that had risen so high in the priesthood, second only to the high priest himself.

Eventually Ulkya's beauty proved to be her undoing as another priest began to pay her attention. She rebuffed his advances but Azull flew into a jealous rage and condemned her to be judged.

Such were the details that spilled forth from the jilted Ulkya. Mortu's impatience bubbled over.

"Tell me how this place works, how we may escape."

She lowered her voice as she continued.

"We cannot. But I know the secrets of the whole wretched cult."

Mortu leaned closer. Over her shoulder she saw the other prisoners seemed to sleep. But Julk looked at the pair with tired eyes.

Ulkya spoke, "Azull was tasked with preparing people for judgement. He was chosen because the high priest thought the secrets of the temple would be safe with him." She ended the sentence with a snort before continuing, "Inside the body of the structure are the pens. Young scorpions are raised from eggs there. In the cool dark they are sluggish, easily controlled. When the heat of the sun hits them, well, it's a different story. Have you seen the ritual? Have you seen people be judged?"

Mortu shook his head no.

"The prisoners are released upon the sands. The priests beseech Daganha for his help in sorting the guilty from the innocent. The pens are opened and the scorpions, Daganha's children, are released. They pause a moment, soaking in the sun. Then they..."

She trailed off. She had seen the ritual perhaps a half dozen times. Despite her faith she found it terrible to behold. And such would be her fate.

Ulkya marshalled her courage. "The children walk among the accused. Many flee, though there is nowhere to go. Others stand still, determined of their innocence. Every time, there is a handful that remain untouched. But the others are torn apart, and consumed."

She shuddered. Her eyes met Mortu's, lit with a sudden fire, a righteous rage.

"But it is a lie! Before the ritual the prisoners receive a blessing from the priests. Each is dabbed with holy oil before they go to the sands. But it is not simple oil. Those the priests deem innocent, those lucky few are dabbed with humors harvested from dead scorpions. The scorpions smell the humors and think the person is one of their own and are spared."

Mortu smirked. "Clever."

"I am glad you are amused. I hope your good mood lasts as you are torn apart."

The barbarian shook his shaggy head. "If that is indeed my fate, then so be it. But until my last breath I will fight."

Ulkya shook her head, overcome with emotion. This man of the North, this strange outlander dared give her a glimmer of hope. She pressed her head to the nape of his corded neck as fresh tears came down her smooth cheeks. He leaned back, gently pressing her shoulders back, forcing her upright.

"No tears, not yet. Tell me of the sands. Tell me of the pens and the arena. Every detail you can recall!"

The party had been long and arduous. Oram's large family and many, many clients had come to show respect to their powerful patron. The dizzying array of faces and cacophony of conversations floated through Kyrus's mind as he lay on a cushion in the dark. Around him, on the carpeted floor and draped across the cushions was a veritable army of toys. They lay where they had fallen as Pinxie had grown bored, strewn like the dead across some fanciful battlefield. The little girl slept in a bed fashioned to resemble a scorpion. A gauzy curtain hung from its arched tail. Kyrus listened to her snore. The little girl had fought sleep like it was death. But the maids had eventually prevailed.

They sat in a servant's room attached to the girl's chambers. Light from an oil lamp painted a warm streak from the door, opened a crack to keep an eye on their charge.

Now that the demands of the evening were over, Kyrus thought only of escape. He hopped to the floor and walked around the room. He tested the door. He winced as the hinges creaked. The snoring continued.

Slowly he poked his head into the dim hallway. One end was a wall. The other stretched on into gloom. He made for the wide balcony next.

From his perch on the rail the city below was a picturesque sprawl. The scorpion loomed over all. From its impressive center the city stretched out in two long arms encircling the bay. Along the left arm was the artisan quarter where only yesterday he played chess. Kyrus peered over the rail. The face of the building was an elaborate working of tiles. They were beautifully painted but unfortunately presented a smooth, featureless surface. Impossible to climb. Far below was another balcony. There was a chance he could let himself drop without injury. But he didn't like the odds. He might use a drape or sheet as rope. The matter required some thought.

He made his way to the maid's room. Three women sat at a low table. From long practice their animated conversation was kept at a low volume so as not to disturb Pinxie. They were stout women, middle aged and bearing the warm amber skin and alluring eyes of the people of the city. They were once concubines and now served as nursemaids after the blush of youth had faded.

"Well, if it isn't Pinxie's newest toy."

Kyrus bowed deeply. "I am Kyrus. At your service, ladies."

The women snickered in between sips of wine and introduced themselves. There was Ataja, Yuna, and Mellia. Ataja had the penetrating eyes of a keen intellect. Yuna and Mellia were of a kind, buxom, and exuding an easy, earthy grace. They both bent at once to snatch up Kyrus. Yuna was faster. She cradled the confused monk in her arms.

"Like a little furry baby."

"And look at his little outfit!"

Next to the woman's bosom Kyrus found himself frozen, unable to speak or move. A moment later the woman mercifully placed him on the table.

Spread in careful columns on the dark wood were beautifully painted cards. Beautiful flowers were rendered in watercolor. Bold reds, oranges, and purples apparently marked suits. Kyrus admired them as he composed himself.

He spoke, "A game, is it, ladies?"

The eldest, Ataja, answered back, "Just a few hands of Urand to pass the time."

"And some wine?" He looked to each in turn. Their big, dark eyes were a touch glassy.

"Yes. Tonight we received a bottle from our master, left over from the party."

"Do you not have wine often?"

"We do not. Slaves are not permitted wine." One of the women pushed her goblet towards Kyrus.

"Very generous!" Kyrus sipped deep.

Mellia asked, "Forgive this question. I can think of more polite way to phrase it. But, what are you?"

Kyrus took a deep breath and launched into the tale of his life. The women sat amused. The strange story was a perfect accompaniment to a late evening of wine and card playing. Finally, the monk told of their two days in the city.

"Somewhere out there my friend Mortu is dead or imprisoned."

The night breeze stirred silk curtains as he looked down at its irregular avenues lit by the soft glow of the insect lamps.

The woman looked at each other. Finally Ataja spoke again.

"I do not wish to upset you, but it is most likely your friend will face judgement tomorrow at the ritual."

Yuna elaborated their theory. "Those wretched priests never stoop to killing in the streets. They prefer to make their enemies stand before Daganha. And it seems that Oram has told them that your friend is an enemy."

Ataja gave her friend a warning look. She leaned towards her companions, beckoning Kyrus close.

"The walls have ears. Watch what you say."

Kyrus spoke, "You heard my tale of courage and perseverance! You must know I intend to escape. I will escape and free my friend as well!" His small fists shot up as he looked towards the heavens. "But how!"

Yuna spoke, "Your ambitions are noble, but even if you manage to get out of here, there is no way to free your friend from the claw."

"There must be some way." Kyrus lifted the goblet to his lips and drank deep. His brow furrowed deeply. He gulped down another mouthful. "This is quite good, actually."

Ataja spoke, "Well, standing here drinking our wine isn't going to get you anywhere. You need knowledge of the claw." She turned to Luna, "You knew a priest or two in your day. And we've all been to the ritual. What do we know of it?"

Luna eyes burned as she spoke. "A priest or two in my day? That's rich coming from the former Queen of the Bayside Quarter."

Mellia interrupted. "Come now, the both of you. This ridiculous creature needs our help."

Luna's anger fled as quickly as it arrived. She sighed as she sank into her cushion, chin resting on her palm. "In truth, I don't think I know anything that could help."

"Nor I."

The women all screamed in unison as the door to the hall flung open. There stood Trunk. In his thick hand he held a whip. The smile across his heavy face was wide.

"So. Pinxie's three witches plot escape and whisper heresy!" With a flick of meaty fingers the whip uncoiled. He licked his lips and spoke, "I'll dole out punishment myself, and spare you all the claw. Such is my mercy."

Kyrus puffed out his chest. "See here now, you odious ogre! These fine women, persons of intellect and character, are aiding me in a righteous task. The liberation of my friend and the righting of a horrible injustice! Remove yourself from this room at once!"

The man froze. He blinked at the monk then a flush came over his smooth flesh.

"You wretched little imp. Make yourself useful and shut the door lest our little party disturb young Pinxie."

"I'll do nothing of the sort!"

The battle of wills ended as Trunk kicked the table, sending Kyrus and the cards flying. With three long strides he crossed the room and shut the door. The maids cried as he tossed them, one by one, to a corner where they could only cower. His eyes burned as he brought the whip back.

Kyrus rose from a pile of playing cards. His legs were small and stringy but powerful relative to his weight. He thought of none of that, nor the incredible gulf between his size and the size of his target. He shot himself like an arrow towards the mad eunuch. Trunk reeled back as Kyrus rained down blows upon his face and eyes, shrieking as he struck, sounding for once like an actual monkey. The big man spun and rebounded from wall to wall as he cursed and growled. His head banged against the lamp hung from chain from the domed ceiling. Mad shadows passed over the women as they watched this bizarre combat unfold. The eunuch could not get a hold of the monk as he danced from neck to head to shoulder and to head again, kicking and punching as he did so. Kyrus got his little hand around one of Trunk's hoop earrings and swung down. The man howled in pain and pitched to the side. An ungainly step, then another and Trunk was engulfed in silk drape. The rail of the balcony loomed forth. Kyrus's eyes went wide as he saw the peril. His small hands grasped at the walls as Trunk stumbled. The noise of the fray gave way to sudden silence as the two were swallowed by the inky night. The women gasped and ran to the edge.

There on the stone, four stories below, Trunk lay still. His neck and head were at odd angles.

Ataja gasped, "The imp! Where is he!"

Tears welled in Luna's eyes. "He died defending us, poor thing!"

"Wait, there!"

Mellia pointed to flash of color, receding in the distance. It was a silk curtain, a swath of bright fabric full of the cool evening air and floating down towards the end of the avenue. A monkey dressed as a prince held its corners.

Mortu and Ulkya sat together, backs leaning against the cool plaster of their irregular cell. The barbarian's mind raced. Ulkya had described in great detail the workings of the Ritual of Preparation and everything she knew about the Great Scorpion, the temple in which they sat. The facts were fascinating and potentially of great use. If only they could win free of the cell. But the door was solid. It failed to budge whatsoever when Mortu had tested his shoulder against it. So confident of its strength, the priests had posted no guard outside, at least none that could be seen from its narrow slit.

There were windows scattered along the curve of the wall but they were high up and slim. Mortu pondered a rush when the door was opened come the morn. He could see no other possibility. He had defeated one of the great scorpions single handed, out in the waste, two mornings ago. But there would be dozens of them tomorrow and he had no weapon. The fatalism of the others in the cell, perhaps three dozen others, disgusted him. He had fought a few battles thought lost before they even began. He had been resigned to death many times. Yet he fought. Such was how the gods' favor could be garnered and victory snatched from the jaws of defeat. The people around him laid or sat on the stone floor, limp with defeat. Doubtless a few might be judged innocent. But it seemed none dared hope. None but Ulkya beside him. Her delicate hands were clenched into fists.

Mortu thought of his friend Kyrus. Where was he? Did he yet live? Did he dwell high up in the paradise which he had blabbed about so frequently? The barbarian hoped that he did, should his time have come.

"Psst!"

The sound came from above. Puzzled, Mortu stood and looked up. There in the window, just tall enough that Mortu could touch the iron brace, was the distinctive silhouette of a small monkey.

"Kyrus!"

"It is I! By God's grace I defeated my captors and made my way here as quick as I could. And I see you are well, though in difficult circumstances."

"Tomorrow we will be killed."

"So I heard."

"Escape seems impossible. But I know the secrets of the temple."

In broad outlines the barbarian relayed the inner workings of the ritual and its preparation.

"That's quite a racket they've got going. The faith of your people is cruel in nature, fickle, and repellent to enlightened people. But this scorpion cult is outright wicked. But first we must get you out of there. I'll find a way in! It will be nothing next to my recent escape! I fought with a great ogre of a man and flew to safety held aloft by a swath of silk!"

Mortu turned to Ulkya. "He frequently exaggerates."

"Bah! I was a savage in battle! I must be spending too much time with you. Tragically it has made you no wiser, but the barbarian in all of us lives closer to the surface in me."

"Kyrus. Dawn will come soon."

"Yes, of course. I will slip into this wretched temple and free you forthwith!"

Kyrus disappeared from view.

Mortu shook his head. "He was enough of a danger to himself before. Gods protect him."

The monk scampered down to the street and ran along the claw's edge. He kept his eyes up, looking for any sort of door. The claw ended and he followed the long length of the arm all the way to where it met the torso. There was a door. Thick iron bands held together stout timbers. Kyrus essayed a gentle tug at the handle. It was locked, as he had expected. But a small window in the wall next to the door was just big enough. Kyrus squeezed through, tumbling onto the cool stone floor. A hallway leading down into the belly of the scorpion was just visible in the gloom. His feet and hands propelled him as fast as he dared. Nowhere in sight was any niche, hole, box, or any article which could offer him a place to hide should someone appear at the other end. His little heart beat in his chest. The rush of recent victory ebbed away faster than he had imagined it would. Kyrus was a tiny thing lost inside a temple of wicked men.

But his friends needed him. The pit in his stomach subsided. He found himself in a square chamber. Each wall had another passage. The right passage would lead towards the head, by his nervous reckoning. He pelted down the passage.

Ahead was light and space. To the left and right of him several doors appeared. They were open. A glance revealed storerooms. Crude crates were stacked atop each other. The smell of cooking assailed his tiny nostrils. Beyond the storerooms there was a kitchen. And past that, the large chamber served as a canteen.

Noise erupted from the kitchen. Kyrus peeked into a room. Several men had entered from a door which led to the storeroom. They bore heavy sacks on their shoulders which they threw on the floor next to a great pot set above a place for fire. One by one they emptied the lentils into the pot. The largest barked an order and a younger man left to return moments later with two large buckets of water.

Kyrus watched as his heart raced. He needed past this door but the men were active, now stirring the lentils while another prepared spices on a thick wooden table. One of them would likely ast not see him skirting past the wide doorway. Beyond he heard more activity in the canteen proper. There was a shout he could not make out and the head cook stuck his head out the door and yelled.

"Breakfast is not for another hour, at least! You keep that foul tongue in your head if you want to eat at all!"

There was no more noise from the canteen. Kyrus was frozen against the wall. Noise now came from whence he had first come, down the long hall. He was trapped. There were men in the canteen ahead and men coming behind.

Move! He had no time. As fast and as low as he could he shot across the hall and into one of the storerooms. He caught the quickest glimpse of the men in the hall. Priests in their ritual regalia, armed and walking with purpose.

One swore. "Scorpion-cursed rats! Gullo! I've warned you before about keeping a clean kitchen! That rat was nearly as big as a cat!"

Behind him a voice quipped. "What do you think he puts in the stew?"

The laughter ended as quick as it had started. From where he had hid, pressing himself between two crates, Kyrus heard the cook groveling. "Begging you pardon. Great and Blessed Azull. Please seat yourself and I shall prepare your tea."

Kyrus sighed in frustration. The temple

was waking. The day of the ritual was a day of much activity. Soon it seemed like dozens of men were in the canteen. The hallway was never without footsteps. Kyrus was trapped.

Ulkya sat against the wall as Mortu paced. He walked amidst the other prisoners, looking them up and down. Above the windows were admitting the warmth of dawn's earliest light.

The barbarian looked down at a merchant. Atop a stained satin shirt, he wore a vest of thick cotton.

"Give me your vest."

The merchant regarded him with fearful eyes. He addressed Ulkya. "What does he say?"

Ulkya relayed the message and the man complied wordlessly.

"Tell him, thanks."

Mortu sat and began tearing the vest into long strips. He would them around his heavy hands until a thick pad protected his palms and wrists.

"What are you doing?"

"It is unlikely we will leave here without facing a blade or two."

Ulkya did not understand but let the matter rest. Outside the door she heard men going to and fro. The preparation for the ritual had begun. Then when the sun was at its zenith and most warming and pleasing to the children of Daganha, then they wound be judged.

"Do you think your friend will find his way to the door and free us?"

Mortu shrugged as he fiddled with the

straps on his hands. "He will or he won't. We shall see. If he is successful we will slip from this place like thieves. Or I might die by spear or scimitar. But I won't be eaten alive. If Kyrus fails I will take many of those priests with me. It's a shame I can't take Dhuden to meet our ancestors. But who knows."

"Azull spoke often of him. Of all the high priests he held only Dhuden in high regard. He is cunning and ruthless. He trains the guards without mercy. His elites bear a tattoo of the scorpion across the face."

"It has been some weeks since I spilled blood in the names of my gods. I know not whether I will live or die. But I know they will be pleased."

There was a sound at the door, metal against metal. Then a creak as the door came open. Mortu's pulse quickened as his muscles tensed.

But it was only a boy, a slave bearing a bucket of water and ladle. Behind him another threw a sack into the cell. The door slammed shut.

The bag contained small loaves of coarse bread. The prisoners distributed the stuff as equitably as they could. Many found themselves unable to eat. Julk, the pious man, paced back and forth, more and more agitated as time passed.

Mortu tore into the loaf Ulkya had gotten for him. He drank a few mouthfuls of water and sat waiting.

The hours of the early morning slipped away. Rays of light descended from high on the wall until they crawled across the floor. The time was coming.

Ulkya wrapped her arms around his chest as the moments slipped by.

Mortu felt sadness in his heart. "Poor Kyrus. He would not flee or give up. They have killed him or captured him." He looked down at his fists. "I know it was not your way, little friend, but I will slay and maim today until I am cut down and go to my ancestors with head high for vengeance is sacred to them."

The door opened.

"We go to the ritual." Ulkya shuddered.

Mortu's muscles tensed. At the mention of the ritual his mind fluttered. The coming rage abated for a moment. He would choose his time carefully and perhaps, if the gods allowed, be given a grand opportunity. He smiled down at Ulkya.

"Stay behind me."

At the door were two priests armed with clubs. At their waists hung swords. Upon their faces were blue- black scorpions.

"Come, all of you! Time to be judged!"

The prisoners shuffled into the hall. At intervals others of the scorpion guard stood, backs against the walls. They pushed the group forward. Malice was written upon their faces as they prodded and struck at the dawdlers. Many had begun to weep and the hallway became a scene of woe. Dejected and broken men and women walked as slow as they dared. Each step a difficulty as they marched towards their fate. Julk walked with head held high. His stiff stride took him to the front of the line. Mortu fell in behind him.

The barbarian affected the gait of the doomed. Though his head was low he scanned constantly. The hallway turned as the arm of the claw joined the torso. The space opened up into a wide chamber. The rafters above were bowed, forming the great golden head of the scorpion. Mortu counted a dozen of the scorpion face men. Milling about the wide chamber were others, some armed, some not. Braziers of fragrant coals filled the air with a sweet smell. The fragrance could not quite mask the acrid smell of scorpion. The space was flooded with bars of bright light from sky-lights cleverly cut into the curves of the mock carapace above. The noise of the assembled crowd outside filled the airy chamber, sounding like running water. The back of the chamber was bars of wrought iron. In the gloom within shapes stirred. Two acolytes with staffs stood by the gate. The prisoners shuffled through the chamber.

Ahead guards stood to form a lane between them. At the end of the lane stood Azull. He was a tall, striking man, dressed in the full regalia required by the ritual. A scorpion fashioned from gold sat upon shoulders layered in black and red silk. Kohl-rimmed eyes looked upon the prisoners with contempt. Behind him a priest stood bearing a slate. On either side were younger acolytes. Each held a stave and at their feet were clay jugs.

Ulkya whispered at Mortu's back. "There it is. The jar on the right contains death. The one on the left contains the humors that make the creatures benign."

From somewhere outside a great bell was wrung. The doom-laden clang silenced the crowd a moment while inside the chamber the priests and the scorpion guards became silent and stood stiffly. At the edges of the room others quickened their steps, hurrying on to whatever errand.

Mortu cleared his mind. He felt his body working through an excess of adrenaline. Like hammering impurities from iron, his muscles were priming themselves for action. His hands were loose at his sides. Soon he would exercise the purpose for which he was born. Violence. He had experienced this moment more times than he could remember. Perhaps today would be the last. Perhaps not. All that mattered was that he fought.

Azull gestured as the Julk stepped forward. His step faltered but he quickly righted himself. Julk looked back. Mortu knew well the look in his eyes. Within the glassy glance was desperate rage and anger. He was a pathetic figure, clothes disheveled and cheeks gaunt. Here was a man betrayed by his beliefs, a victim of his own faith.

The priest intoned a litany and then turned to the boy on the right. The young man dipped the stave into the jar and then touched it to the man's chest. The stuff was odorless and clear but had a strange, frothy quality. As Mortu pondered it events began of their own accord.

From Julk's cracked lips issued a shrill scream as the man knocked aside the stave and leapt towards the Master of the Rite of Preparation.

"Fraud!" he screamed as his hands sought the priest's neck with desperate fury. A club smashed him down and then another.

Mortu wasted no time. The gods had sent this boon, this distraction, and he would not let it go to waste. All eyes were on Julk.

The barbarian struck the closest guard with a vicious hook that crushed bone and sent the man crumpling to the ground. He dropped another before a cry from the next in line spurred his fellows to action. Behind him the other prisoners reeled back in an ungainly scramble. Azull's eyes were wide with alarm as he shouted.

"Blades for this one! Dhuden warned us he would be trouble!"

Practiced motions brought blades from scabbards and the guards advanced toward Mortu. He ducked a slash and kicked his attacker, sending him flying. A trio of guards were toppled. The barbarian caught the next cut in his hands. He grinned at the man's shock. Mortu wrenched the blade free with a sharp twist. He kicked again, hearing the sickening sound of cartilage snapping in the man's knee. He flipped the blade in the air and caught the handle.

The game was different now. He yelled as he slashed and backslashed, felling two men and coming before Azull.

The high priest scrambled backwards. His hands fumbled at the sword at his waist. But Azull was too lofty a figure in the priesthood to waste his time on the training ground. Finally the blade won free. Mortu slashed mightily. The steel cut through the high priest's wrists. He fell to his knees as thick blood pumped from the stumps. His scream was cut short by a downward slash that found where neck and shoulder met. There was a jet of dark red and the man collapsed fully.

The chamber was chaos. Scorpion guards were being dragged underneath the vengeful mob. Merchants, tradesmen, laborers, wives and mothers, pummeled the guards under a torrent of clumsy blows. Not even the acolytes were spared. Mortu smiled. He inspected his blood-drenched blade.

"This is good steel."

He felt something at his back and spun around to find Ulkya. She wrapped her arms around him.

"We live, still."

"We do. For now. There are many more priests and guards about."

"Ho there! What a mess you've made!"

The familiar voice sounded from above. Mortu looked to the rafters.

"Kyrus! You have decided to join us."

A small, furry face grinned down at the

barbarian.

"I was unfortunately delayed. The temple became a beehive soon after I left on my errand. Now that things are underway the halls were again deserted. And here I am. It seems I missed one of your famous displays of bad temper."

Mortu looked around. The guards and priests lay dead. The prisoners were all looking at the barbarian. Alarm showed on their peaked faces.

The barbarian's voice filled the chamber. "Rather than stare like sheep, arm yourselves. Soon they will realize something amiss. We'll have to face the lot of them."

Kyrus made his way down from the rafters. He stared at the jugs, scratching his chin.

"Perhaps we won't."

Mortu looked out of the yawning scorpion's mouth. There was the expanse of sand, hazy in the heat. Just visible across the field was the gallery where the high priests and their many attendants presided over the ceremony. The barbarian looked down at the jar.

He turned to Kyrus. "I believe we are thinking the same thing."

Mortu addressed the prisoners. "Anyone who desires escape, do so now! Find your way out through the bowels of the temple."

Ulkya stood over Azull's corpse. Across her face was a look of malicious satisfaction. Mortu took her arm and pushed her toward the passageway where others had begun to disappear.

"Your knowledge has given us a great opportunity. Now, go to your family, be safe."

She nodded and joined the other prisoners.

Mortu took up the jug containing the benign humor. He took a handful and rubbed in on his sweat and blood-stained chest.

"Can you open the gates?"

Kyrus stood in the far corner next to an iron mechanism.

"Pulling this lever releases counterweights."

Mortu looked at the men. "If the woman mistook one jar for the other, then we will be torn apart." He took Azull's robe from his bloody body. He then bent and retrieved the jar of the substance that would provoke the arachnids. Gingerly he placed the jar inside and grasped the ends, forming a sling of sorts.

"If she was right then the priests will soon know the wrath of their god."

The men nodded.

The barbarian stood at the open mouth. At his feet the shade of the chamber ended and brilliant sunlight found the glitter in the sand. He took a deep breath.

Mortu turned to his friend. "Open the gates!"

Dhuden surveyed the crowd from the shade of the priest's gallery. Great swathes of iridescent silk were stretched over bamboo frames that swayed in the bay-scented wind. The priest's gallery was the highest elevation in the temple-stadium. To his left sat the high priest, Ghumil The Wise and Eternally Blessed.

People said he was near 100 years old, and certainly looked it, by Dhuden's reckoning. Dry skin the texture of parchment, taut over frail bones, poked out from the embroidered sleeves of his silk robes. The old man's smoky eyes looked down at the audience with satisfaction.

"Good crowd, today."

Dhuden replied, "Yes, Blessed One." And then turned away so the high priest could not see his smirk. The galleries surrounding the sands could seat 20,000. Hours before the ritual the corps of guards would fan out around the city, gathering spectators. When the streets were bare they would knock on doors. None could refuse.

The galleries near the priests' area were packed with the indigents. Skins of wine were provided and passed around along with loaves of hearty bread. These spectators enjoyed their repast on the condition that they be vocal in their passion for the ritual. Guards with short whips encouraged the lax. Fanning outwards the galleries were full of whoever the guards found. Priests stalked the aisles to monitor for signs of wavering faith.

Dhuden smiled. It was all his doing. He had unlocked the potential of the cult of Daganha. His priests ruled the city. When the frail old man was finally dead he would replace him as high priest. Then his ambitions could blossom properly, beyond the sun baked walls of this charming city. He flicked his fingers and an acolyte came forward with a goblet of cool water flavored with a citrus. From a silver tray he took a morsel, a locust covered in spice. Another flick brought him a moistened towel. The acolytes scattered at an order from a priest sitting at Ghumil's left. The sun was high. The shadow of the tail lay across its golden head.

The high priest stood with the aid of two acolytes. He raised his hands and began the invocations. Below, on the flanks of the priests' gallery, his words were repeated by deep-throated men. Their voices filled the hot air.

The hard men near the priests began to bay savagely in anticipation. Soon the accused would be judged. Most would be found wanting. And then the savage sport would begin. Most of the men and women would run madly though there was nowhere to hide, nowhere to escape. One by one the children of Daganha would bring them down. Great claws would pin them as the stingers came down. The poison was not a mercy. Limbs paralyzed the victims would still feel everything of what came next.

Dhuden smiled.

Behind a great bell was struck. The high priest sat down but the criers continued to chant. A line of priests in the front row began another chant in harmony. Drums began to beat a slow tattoo. The ritual was building. A well of primal ecstasy began to rise in the hearts of the faithful while those without such sentiment began to fear for the grisly spectacle. Others waited with black lust.

Dhuden waited for the first of the accused to step out onto the sands.

The moments went by, each longer than the next.

After a time, he could see priests looking at each other, asking, wondering. A delay was highly irregular.

Dhuden growled. "Mortu…"

The high priest looked down at him. "What's that?"

"Mortu!"

Across the sands a single figure had emerged from the shadowy mouth. He was tall and powerfully built. Blood stained his bare chest. On long strides the man ran towards the priest's gallery. The shadows from the cruel sun above made his face a grim mask. The crowd fell silent. The barbarian carried a sword in one hand and a bundle in the other.

Dhuden cursed as he made for the edge of the gallery, pushing his fellow priests aside. He shouted to his guards.

"To me!"

On the sands Mortu had stopped. He let the fabric of the bundle play out and then began to swing it in great arcs above his head. His arms and hard torso strained with the effort. When it could spin no faster he gave a great yell and let loose.

The jar slipped from the silk and soared high, landing with a great crash in the center of the priests' gallery. The frothy stuff spattered far.

Dhuden and his men let themselves drop from the edge of the gallery. They landed heavily upon the sands and drew their steel. Above them the gallery was in chaos. The ritual of preparation was an open secret amongst the priests. The panic spread like wildfire. Some were drenched in the stuff. Others had been untouched but brushed against their fellows.

On the sands Mortu stood with his blade. Dhuden and his men ran towards him.

There was a strange shriek and suddenly the scorpions poured forth from the mouth of the temple built in their horrible image.

Screams of fear erupted from the priest's gallery. The horde of skittering claws and tails washed over Mortu like waves in the surf. He stood and smiled as the guards recoiled in their haste to avoid the terrible tide.

But Dhuden was unphased. He was untouched by the humors and unafraid of the creatures. Indeed, he felt an affinity for them, an emotion as close to affection as one like him could feel.

The guards scattered. Some attempted to scale the sheer wall back to the gallery. They were the first to be set upon. The scorpions were made mad by such a concentration of the liquid. The air was heavy with it. The closer they came the more desirous of blood they became. They chattered and shrieked as the screams of the dying rang out. The creatures scaled the wall with ease, clambering over each other in their haste.

They fell upon the priests in a terrible rage. They were beyond the impulse to consume. They wanted only to rend flesh and break bone, to tear their prey apart and find another and then another. The exit from the priest's area became choked with men, scratching and kicking each other. Men became animals as they screeched and cried and desperately sought escape. The high priest was abandoned. Three arachnids fell upon him at once, tearing and pulling and finally tossing the old man's limbs into the air trailing arcs of glistening gore.

The priests fled vainly throughout the galleries. The scorpions were soon amongst the spectators, the once enthusiastic crowd reeling.

And on the sands Mortu and Dhuden faced each other.

"You've made a mess of things."

"It was my pleasure."

The men began to circle each other. They were of identical build and possessed wide experience of combat. Both came from warrior stock, manipulated by the old masters. Mortu had the advantage of a man with nothing to lose. He had a woman waiting for him. And at night sometimes he was beset with visions of leading an army. Those things seemed far away now. In this moment he owned nothing but the blood-stained blade in his hand. Dhuden stood amidst the wreckage of careful and ruthless ambition. But the priest was older and wiser.

The priest screamed and lunged forward. Mortu saw the feint and gave up a few feet of ground. Sparks danced across the blades' edges as the barbarian parried away Dhuden's backslash. The priest brought the blade back with a smooth motion then thrust. Mortu knocked the blow aside and stepped forward. Dhuden got his blade up just in time to parry a vicious downwards cut. The pair were too close now for fancy bladework. Mortu sent his elbow into Dhuden's face. A torrent of red erupted from his crushed nose. From the corner of his eye the barbarian spied a glint of steel below. He shifted as pain erupted along his side and he reeled back, kicking.

The priest held a dagger in his off hand. He smiled through a mask of hate and dark blood.

The jagged cut bit deep into Mortu's ribs. Had he not shifted the blade would have found his lungs. The priest pressed his advantage, rushing at his foe with a flurry of blows. The blade came down again and again while the dagger struck out like a viper. Mortu met blade with blade and turned and ducked to avoid the dagger. Dhuden was strong and fast. The barbarian gave up more steps as the priest pressed the attack.

His face glowed with furious rage and the anticipation of bloody victory as Mortu reeled.

The barbarian's heel seemed to catch and

he stumbled backwards. Dhuden screamed and lunged, bringing his blade high.

Mortu let his sword slip out of his hand. He caught Dhuden's wrist and pulled him down as his legs shot up. Dhuden was pitched end over end. Mortu followed him.

He straddled the priest now. Before Dhuden could react, Mortu's fist struck down. The first blow stunned the priest. A torrent followed.

There on the hot sands of the temple to Daganha, Mortu, of the Men of the North, beat to death his countryman, the wicked priest known as Dhuden.

Mortu stood above the lifeless body and looked around at the carnage. The priest's gallery and much of the nearby area had become a gore-soaked charnel house. The other galleries were empty. The frenzy was ebbing. The scorpions were now gorging themselves.

"I thought he had you." Kyrus gestured to the corpse with its ruined head and face.

"The sands called to mind a trick from the arenas in Zantyum. Dhuden's mind started thinking of victory. In such a state one is vulnerable to ploys and ruses."

Kyrus surveyed the stands. "I had hoped these people, the priests, would someday turn away from their ways. Alas, they will never have the opportunity."

Mortu shrugged. "The gods are never more generous than when they give people what they deserve."

Kyrus looked around furtively then made a

quick search of Dhuden's robes. With a noise of triumph, he produced a bag of coin, quite heavy in his little hands.

"I am hot, hungry, and tired. I suggest we refresh ourselves somewhere and leave as soon as we can. Who knows if someone will want revenge for this calamity or not."

"I agree. But we have one more errand. The iron steed still ails. And there are debts to be paid." Mortu looked down at his friend. A look of puzzlement appeared on his bronze face. "Kyrus. Why are you wearing that ridiculous costume?"

"It was for my wedding. I was married last evening to a Duchess, a doll, in fact. The wedding was planned and overseen by Oram's granddaughter."

Mortu's hearty laugh echoed across the hot sand. "So you are married now."

"Hardly. The ceremony was not the Catholic rite."

Oram sat in his spacious office. A light breeze from the bay windows stirred the papers strewn across the wide desk of dark wood. Its surface was covered with gems, coins, and rare treasures from all over the world. At his right hand was a crystal box containing an ancient timepiece, the last extant example of the work of Master Swodeck. In the far corner sat an ancient green box bearing a bank of buttons. A cable led to a wand topped with a bulb of wire mesh. Into this device Oram's secretary, a harried man in rumpled robes, spoke while pressing another device close to his ear. Papers lay everywhere about the office; deeds written in looping script granted the bearer stock in trading companies, mining concessions, all manner of things. Via the rare machine Oram was conferring with the managers of his affairs west, the line of trade that linked Kwarzim to far Zanytum and Oscogn in the north. At Oram's right sat a pensive man, reed thin, bald. He sat with legs crossed while he examined his fingernails.

Huj, flanked by two limping guards, interrupted the conference.

"My lord. A man is here with a proposal." Blood ran from his split lips as he talked.

"By Daganha! What has happened to you!" Oram stood. His impressive bulk towered over his confederates.

"Begging your pardon, my lord. I was instructed to relay this message to avoid further harm to my person. It goes as follows: you, my lord, have incurred a blood debt against Mortu, warrior of the north. You will grant him his choice of items amongst your stock of bright iron, as well as 100 pieces of gold. Otherwise, Mortu will kill you and your family, so that your dishonorable seed will never again inconvenience honorable men."

Oram stood still, mouth open. He sputtered a moment then addressed the guards flanking his beleaguered aid.

"Is he capable of such a thing."

The guard to Huj's left winced as he nodded. His left eye was swollen shut. "Yes, my lord. I believe so. It is said he was responsible for the fiasco at the temple."

"Well, that is something." He looked to his advisor, the thin man next to him.

The man spoke softly, "A hundred isn't too dear. And if the priests are laid low we will save much coin. The bright iron can be spared."

Oram looked at Huj. "Do it. And clean yourself up before you think to interrupt me again."

Huj sighed in relief. He bowed and left.

Two days later Thogon and his family bade Mortu and Kyrus goodbye at the gate of the city. The family was ebullient with the windfall provided by the strange pair. The barbarian had expressed regret that he could not have paid Thogon more. The artificer had fixed the heart of the iron steed and it thundered as well as it ever had. Thogon looked around. The city was on edge. The ruining of the temple had left a vacuum. In the piazza, workplace, and homes people argued about their faith and their future. Some wished to reinstate the cult, though curbing its more aggressive tendencies. Others argued that Daganha needed no cult, no priesthood, and could be best honored by offerings in the home. A small group, Thogon among them, spoke of a cult from the west, something new though it was once old, some of the old ways nearly destroyed by the alien masters. The people knew little of this cult, only what Kyrus had told them.

Of Mortu they spoke little. Amongst those that would keep to the old faith he would be remembered. He was the chosen of Daganha who delivered judgement to those that did evil in his name. Tall and powerful, with a demonic mien and savage ability, Mortu lurked in dark places, waiting to punish the wicked.

Bury yourself in....

Pilum Press No. 2
Available Spring 2022
www.pilumpress.com

RETVRN

Pilum Press Trade Edition
Kickstarter in 2022
www.pilumpress.com

Sex, Books,

& SHAGDUK

a novel of 1977

jb jackson

Kickstarter, Spring 2022 pilumpress.com